Exploring Dark Short Fiction #2: A Primer to Kaaron Warren

Anthologies Edited by Eric J. Guignard

A World of Horror (forthcoming) (Dark Moon Books, 2018)

After Death... (Dark Moon Books, 2013)

Dark Tales of Lost Civilizations (Dark Moon Books, 2012)

The Five Senses of Horror (Dark Moon Books, 2018)

+Horror Library+ Volume 6 (Cutting Block Books/ Farolight Publishing, 2017)

Pop the Clutch: Thrilling Tales of Rockabilly, Monsters, and Hot Rod Horror (forthcoming) (Dark Moon Books, 2018)

Exploring Dark Short Fiction (A Primer Series) Created by Eric J. Guignard

#1: A Primer to Steve Rasnic Tem (Dark Moon Books, 2017)

#2: A Primer to Kaaron Warren (Dark Moon Books, 2018)

#3: A Primer to Nisi Shawl (forthcoming) (Dark Moon Books, 2018)

#4: A Primer to Jeffrey Ford (forthcoming) (Dark Moon Books, 2018)

Written by Eric J. Guignard

Baggage of Eternal Night (JournalStone, 2013)

Crossbuck 'Bo (forthcoming, 2019)

That Which Grows Wild: 16 Tales of Dark Fiction (forthcoming) (Cemetery Dance Publications, 2018)

EXPLORING DARK SHORT FICTION #2: A PRIMER TO KAARON WARREN

EDITED BY ERIC J. GUIGNARD

COMMENTARY BY MICHAEL ARNZEN, PhD

ILLUSTRATIONS BY MICHELLE PREBICH

DARK MOON BOOKS
Los Angeles, California

Edited by Eric J. Guignard
Cover design by Eric J. Guignard
www.ericjguignard.com
Commentary by Michael Arnzen, PhD
www.gorelets.com
Interior illustrations by Michelle Prebich
www.batinyourbelfry.etsy.com

First edition published in May, 2018
Library of Congress Control Number: 2018932287
ISBN-13: 978-0-9989383-0-1 (paperback)
ISBN-13: 978-0-9989383-3-2 (e-book)

DARK MOON BOOKS
Los Angeles, California
www.DarkMoonBooks.com
Made in the United States of America

This book is dedicated to those who encourage the written word, those who seek a deeper understanding of literature, and those who simply love dark fiction.

And of course, this is dedicated also to Kaaron Warren, an inspiration to so many. Thank you for consenting to this project.

To all you writers, can't wait to see your stories in print!

Kaaron Warren
grand Rapids
2019

TABLE OF CONTENTS

INTRODUCTION

BY ERIC J. GUIGNARD

THE COMMONWEALTH OF AUSTRALIA IS AN exercise in disparities, a country both bleak and beautiful, rugged while idealized, urbane yet still untamed, and has produced some of the greatest literary authors of the 20th and 21st centuries, with names coming to mind such as Mary Gilmore, Patrick White, Thomas Keneally, Tim Winton, and Peter Carey, amongst others, and notwithstanding the subject of this book: Kaaron Warren.

Kaaron's writing, like her native homeland, is filled with similar seeming disparate affectivities: rich passion turning to cruel heartache, bitter catastrophe preceding joyful triumph, ebullience until emotional devastation, all in storylines that wend, at their leisure, along a path of subtle life hues, often set in domestications from which a character is thrust or encounters those vagaries of fate that are to be most feared.

And she seems oft to manage it all within the span of only a few brief pages.

Widely hailed as one of Australia's—and the world's—premiere writers today of speculative and dark fiction, Kaaron Warren has published four novels, multiple novellas, five collections, essays, and well over one hundred heart-rending tales of horror, science fiction, and beautiful fantasy, and is the first author ever to simultaneously win all three of Australia's top speculative fiction writing awards (Ditmar, Shadows, and Aurealis awards for *The Grief Hole*).

Her award-winning short fiction regularly appears in anthologies, magazines, and other publications across the U.S., Europe, and Australia as well as being reprinted routinely in *Year's Best* compilations. Her short story "A Positive" has been made into the short film, *Patience*, and her first-ever published short story "White Bed" was dramatized for the stage.

And, for all she has accomplished, Kaaron is still easily accessible to fans, willing to help others, and, quite simply, a joy to work with, particularly that she was kind enough to participate in this project, the second *Primer* designed to showcase diverse modern voices around the world of leading dark fiction short stories.

Author and journalist Lucius Shepard, in his introduction to *Dead Sea Fruit* (2010), regaled Kaaron also as spanning of disparities, a foremost example of those who can bridge the constrictive labels between "Stylist" and "Storyteller," describing her prose as "holding a profound sway over his emotions." For lack of expressing anything more eloquently, I repeat his sentiment; this because I love great stories and, more, I love great stores that are unique in the way they're told, and, even more than that, I love great and unique stories that can make me *feel*.

Although Kaaron Warren has been writing published fiction for over a quarter century, it wasn't until about 2010 or 2011 that I encountered her work. One of her first short stories I read was in a second-hand science fiction anthology that was given to me by an ex-felon acquaintance who was in rehab for drug addiction. He used both substance abuse and science fiction as "escapes from life," but while one means gave him hope toward something invigorating in the future, the other ultimately killed him. That book contained Kaaron's tale, "Ghost Jail," and perhaps because of its subject—tortured ghosts and those tortured living who can see them, along with the search for redemption, for peace—and *who* the book came from, the writing struck me very deeply. It was surreal and meaningful, multi-voiced and, ultimately, about that very struggle to escape poor circumstances, to find freedom, peace.

Shortly thereafter I read "All You Can Do Is Breathe," which is emotionally wrecking, yet the trauma comes subtly, by the loss of the ability to find joy in life, in this narrative by something out of the protagonist's control: a haunting, sucking creature. Much the same for "The Edge of a Thing," which by its ending, a wealthy and loved father is promised to lose all by a wronged ghost: "Your son's seed will be poison. Your daughter will be barren. We wish great unhappiness to your family. Your wife will come to hate you as the mongoose hates the snake. You will not be an ancestor."

Passages such as those bring me bitter despair.

And yet there are joyful stories by Kaaron too, beautiful reflections, such as the hopeful and compassionate "The Speaker of Heaven," the sweet fairy tale-esque "Born and Bread," and the beautifully redemptive "Death's Door Café."

So it is that the disparities in our surrounds, in our lives, in ourselves, are able—at their best and their worst—to be captured by Kaaron Warren.

Midnight cheers,

—Eric J. Guignard
Chino Hills, California
January 29, 2018

ABOUT KAARON WARREN

MY SHADOW EXISTENCE:
AN AUTOBIOGRAPHICAL ACCOUNT

FOR MOST OF MY LIFE I'VE CARRIED ALONG A shadow existence. Many of us do: that other self, the one most people don't see. We present a public face to the world, that is the public existence.

Then there is the face most people don't see. Sometimes those secrets are large and never to be revealed. Sometimes, we realize people knew the truth all along.

My shadow existence as a child was twofold. I lied every single day about my religious background, and I wanted to be a writer. I *did* write, novels and short stories I told no one about, confessed to no one, scrawling them by hand onto scavenged paper, scraps, and notes I still have, or had, until a rat died in a box stored in the shed.

My religious background was unusual and not something anyone would understand in suburban Melbourne, where I grew up. It was weird enough we were vegetarians, something I couldn't hide. That alone got me noticed. But the other stuff?

I didn't tell a soul.

Things I remember: A first kiss in the Bay at South Melbourne while my family were chanting Hare Krishna in the ashram a few blocks away. This boy saying, "Are you one of those *vegitaryists*?" when I told him I didn't eat meat, and, when he saw two Hare Krishna women walk past in saris, he said, "I hate those people." Me saying nothing because I didn't feel I belonged to them. They were in my shadow existence. I started writing my first novel around this time. Red ink in exercise books, about prejudice and teen gangs and violence. I used everything I saw, translated into story on the page, but not the stuff that was actually happening. Not the huge feasts and the chants, the hours spent making flower necklaces for the gods (and that smell still makes me sleepy, the smell of chrysanthemums, because I was so tired making those necklaces). All of this annoying, more than anything else, let me be clear. None of it abusive.

Soon after I spent time in New Zealand on a Hare Krishna farm. They had me collecting money for them on the streets of Auckland but we didn't say that, we said we were collecting for teenagers on drugs or something, so there was a shadow self within my shadow self. I kept a diary at the time for my best friend, every last bit of it a lie. I lied about where I was staying, what I did all day. While my friends were swimming in the lake or sleeping all day, I was getting up at 4 a.m., dressing in a sari, being told that I was disturbing the bachelors so I needed to cover up even more. I was eating delicious food, sleeping on the floor of a caravan, writing letters homes to friends that didn't describe the filthy unemptied portable toilets, left for days past the time they should be collected because the contractor didn't like the Hare Krishnas.

I was being called a prostitute by a man who worked on the top floor of one of the offices. Apparently watching me collect money made him very angry, although why he was staring down at a fourteen-year-old on the street he didn't say.

All of it grist for the mill. All of it stories in the making. I still get caught sometimes using shadow existence terminology in life and in my stories. Words like "take rest" and "isn't it." Words stick with me, like the guru telling us that the only pure pleasure was passing stool.

I wrote a story called "The Animodes Revolt" at this time,

inspired by a piece of equipment at my grandmother's house. When I was at her house I was myself; no shadow required. My absolute self. She knew about the religion. She knew I wanted to be a writer.

Before the Hare Krishnas there was Transcendental Meditation. Lots of blessed-out, very kind adults. What I remember: The apple crumble they all brought to Pot Luck Suppers. The stink of one of the women, who wore a particular kind of shirt, nylon, flowery. Whenever I see a shirt like that at a second-hand clothing shop I think of her and her stink.

The tedium of meditation. It was boring, as an eight-year-old, sitting still for twenty minutes, so I wrote stories in my head.

The night I remember the most, although I may have dreamt it, is the night after the day my bedroom was used to initiate a record number of people. Thirty, maybe? Forty? A lot. My room was full of incense, and cleaner that it had ever been, and white cover on the bed that was new for me. But that night, I was riven with nightmares. Dreams and visions of things flying. And I wonder, I really do, if all of that poured out of the people being initiated. All their stories floating around and entering me. When people ask me where my stories come from, sometimes I'm tempted to tell them *there. In that room.* I'm writing the stories of all of those people, which is why my characters can seem alive. They are alive. They were.

For a while I stopped thinking I was a writer. No, I always wrote, but I stopped thinking I'd ever succeed. I wrote dozens of stories in this time, all typed up on an electronic typewriter.

My shadow self, believing in itself even when I didn't.

I moved with my family from Melbourne to Sydney. I thought at the time I wanted to work in advertising, and I did for a while. I thought I wanted to be a copy writer but realized quickly that it would take all my ideas, all of my fictional thoughts. So I edited video tape in a studio in the basement of the agency, and I wrote stories there, novels, snippets, notes, and ideas, all of it on scraps of paper, scrounged notebooks, many thousands of words.

I met the man who'd become my husband, who still is my husband, and we moved to Canberra together.

You find that when you move to a new place, you are the person you are at the moment you arrive. You aren't the old person, the other person, you are *that* person. So when I arrived in Canberra, I decided I'd be a writer. We moved for my husband's job, so I had to be sure I had an identity of my own or be lost in it all. So I was a writer, and soon I sold my first short story (1993, "White Bed," in *Shrieks: A Horror Anthology*, Women's Redress Press). We travelled back to Sydney for the book launch and I read the opening to the story, my knees shaking so much the hem of my dress vibrated.

Then children came along and the writer self sank into the shadows again. People wanted to talk about babies and sleep and feeding and mashed pumpkin, about which school and where on holidays. I did write during those early years, though, snatching moments when I could. Using the many hours we spent watching trucks to *think*, to observe, to fill myself with images and ideas. I published during this time and won my first award, the Aurealis Award for Short Horror Fiction ("A Positive" first published in *Bloodsongs* magazine). This kept me going through it all. I love the 'mother' part of my existence, but the importance of maintaining the 'writer' part of my existence can't be underestimated.

In Fiji there was a new kind of shadow existence. We went for three years for my husband's job, so we were in the diplomatic corps. I was a 'trailing spouse,' so-called. But I was a writer, too. I explored the town of Suva, I spoke to people, and I wrote and wrote and wrote. I finished two novels there and dozens of short stories. I sold my first three novels (*Slights*, *Walking the Tree*, and *Mistification*, to Angry Robot Books). I hosted dinners for people from many countries, I made abiding friendships with fascinating people, and I listened, observed, absorbed.

We're back in Canberra now. Life isn't always an adventure but I try to find adventure in small things. In my interactions and observations of people. In finding treasures like a small box of bus tickets from 1993, collected by someone. Each journey a note of this person's existence.

When my husband got very sick a couple of years ago (he is well now), someone said, *you'll have to give up being a writer* and I thought, *no*. It actually did me some damage, her saying this, but I am about 80% writer. It's so much a part of my identity that I don't know who I'd be otherwise. What I'd do. What I'd think about. How I'd spend my spare moments if I wasn't reading odd books for ideas for stories, or constantly observing the world around me.

I've been a writer for most of my life and some parts flash at me, images that influenced my writing even though I can find no trace of them in any story.

Which makes me realize that my shadow self is not shadow any more. The writer is flesh.

So who is the shadow now?

A BIOGRAPHY

KAARON WARREN PUBLISHED HER FIRST SHORT story in 1993 and has had stories in print every year since. She has lived in Melbourne, Sydney, Canberra, and Fiji, She's sold many short stories, four novels (the multi-award-winning *Slights*, *Walking the Tree*, *Mistification*, and *The Grief Hole*), and six short story collections. Her most recent novel, *The Grief Hole*, won the

ACT Writers and Publisher's Award, a Canberra Critic's Circle Award for Fiction, a Ditmar Award, the Australian Shadows Award, and the Aurealis Award. Her stories have appeared in Australia, the US, the UK, and elsewhere in Europe, and have been selected for both Ellen Datlow's and Paula Guran's *Year's Best* anthologies.

Her next novel will come out in 2018 from Omnium Gatherum Books.

She has recent stories in Ellen Datlow's *Mad Hatters and March Hares*, *Looming Low* from Dim Shores, Nate Pedersen's *Sisterhood*, Cemetery Dance's *Dark Screams* series, and *Bitter*, a novella, from Cemetery Dance.

Kaaron was a Fellow at the Museum for Australian Democracy, where she researched prime ministers, artists, and serial killers. In 2018 she will be Established Artist in Residence at Katharine Susannah Prichard House in Western Australia. She's taught workshops in haunted asylums, old morgues, and second-hand clothing shops, and she's mentored several writers through a number of programs.

Kaaron works two days a week in a second-hand bric-a-brac shop, which provides her with endless ideas for stories.

She will be Guest of Honor at the World Fantasy Convention in 2018, New Zealand's Lexicon 2019, and StokerCon in Michigan in 2019.

You can find her at http://kaaronwarren.wordpress.com, Instagram is kaaron_warren, and she Tweets @KaaronWarren.

GUARDING THE MOUND

ONE OF THE BOYS CAME BACK A MAN, HIS ARMS
marked, his feet cut and bloody.

Din looked on as the boy, now a new man, showed the stone
he had sharpened and used to kill the meal they would all share.
Nobody noticed Din.

"I'll go out next," Din said. "I'm old enough." He said it
loudly and often until the new man noticed. "Din, you stay with
the women. You cannot be a man when you are the size of a
child." Everybody laughed, slapped Din, slapped the new man.
Din crouched down and crawled through their legs to get out
into the night air. Someone smacked his arse and said, "Hi ho,
little Din," and he turned to snarl but no one noticed, no one
cared.

"I'll do it," he said. He stood by the entrance to his
underground home and took up a sharp stick. He scratched
markings into his arms and legs. Then he began to run.

The animal howls were louder at night. The noise of them
frightened him but he knew that was part of the test. He
wondered what he was supposed to do next.

The moon shone a path and Din began to follow it. He felt no
hunger; his belly was full of the new man's feast.

He walked, enjoying the freedom.

The moon stayed bright and Din walked till he was tired. He
found a stone along the way and chipped at it till it was sharp.
Then he found a hollow tree and hid inside behind its branches,

waiting for a kill to come. His eyes drooped and the warm air inside the trunk made him sleepy, so sleepy . . .

He awoke with the sun in his eyes to the sound of voices and smiled, thinking his people had come to look for him.

Then he heard them speak and realized by their accent they were strangers. Din scrunched his eyes tight, thinking they wouldn't see him if he curled up small.

"Look at the size of him," a man said. They poked him with a stick.

"Child."

"I'm not," Din could not help but answer.

They laughed.

"Of course you're a child."

"I am a man," said Din. He held his arms out, showing the deep, fresh marks there.

"Only just, hey?"

"Look at the size of him," someone said again. Din shrank back.

"It's all right. No need to fear. We are hunting animals, not you. Why don't you climb out?"

"I'll wait for my family."

The men talked amongst themselves. Then one of them said to Din, "Are you from the moles who lived underground?"

Din gasped at the insult. "It is safe there. The animals don't get us."

"But it's dangerous living underground. You're safe from wild animals but someone could just come and cover the entrance. How would you get out?"

Din heard them sheathing their weapons. He cautiously moved forward.

"Are your weapons away?"

"You're very observant, boy."

"I'm not a boy."

Din heard the sound of someone drinking.

"Do you have water?"

"We do, my friend. Plenty to share. And meat, too."

Din cautiously climbed out of the tree. He saw six tall men with dirty faces, brown arms.

"Good for you," said one. "Brave." He patted Din on the back. He smelled of burned meat, blood. "I am the Chieftain's Man. I know bravery. Are you hungry, my friend? Come share with us." Din shared their meat.

"He's very small," said one of the men.

"My father grew not much bigger. I will stay small, too," said Din. He felt brave to say the words, to accept the words.

"And what job do you expect to take?"

"I am very patient. I can watch the lake for the moment the ice cracks. I can watch the sky for the sign of breaking rain. I can watch a sick face for a sign of fever breaking."

The men exchanged glances. One of them said, "Tell me of your people," and Din told them of his home, how close it was. How enclosing and how the people talked little. He could hear the Chieftain's Man talking a distance away. "He seems perfect."

"You would say that. Otherwise your son is in line. Your son will be starved to keep him small."

"I know."

Din heard a catch in the Chieftain's Man's voice.

"The Chieftain will not be happy you have used his time for your own gain."

"Spoils of war," the Chieftain's Man said. He came back to Din.

Din said, "My family don't think much of me. They didn't think I could become a new man."

Din's new friend said, "That's no good, boy. You should come with us. You are brave and strong, Din. We need someone like you. We don't hide underground like moles. We have built houses on the earth. The air we breathe at night is fresh."

He put his arm around Din. "I'm the Chieftain's Man and I have his ear. He'll be happy to see you. You should join with us, my friend. Our place is big with plenty of people to talk to. You might like it."

Din blinked. "My people would miss me."

"They might. But would you miss them?"

Din shrugged. "They're my family."

The men exchanged glances again. The Chieftain's Man said, "I'll confide in you. We are hunting animals and we are seeking treasures. Power." He stood over Din, muscles flexing, blood in his fingernails. "Our Chieftain sent us out to destroy those we find. He is frightened of invasion. You family, Din . . . I'm sorry. But they were like ants, under there. Underground. We just covered up the hole and left them there. They probably just fell asleep."

The Chieftain's Man nodded his head, closed his eyes, dropped his head to his chest, aping sleep.

"Yet you, young man, are alive. By your own actions you saved your life."

Din felt full to his ears. "My mother?" he said.

"Did anybody call for Din as they were buried?" asked the Chieftain's Man.

"No. Nobody called for him. They called plenty of names, but I didn't hear Din."

Din suspected they were tricking him, that perhaps they wanted him for some purpose of their own. But he did not want to go back to find his family smothered. And he wanted to live above ground, with people who thought he was brave, and strong, and useful.

He liked his life with them. He was always much smaller but they didn't notice so much. The Chieftain enjoyed his talk and laughed at him, and Din felt he had a place to be.

Din was uneasy when the Chieftain's Man came to measure him.

"I know I'm short but you don't need to make such a point of it," he said, slapping the man's hand away. "Get that rope away from me. I'm shorter than a man and taller than a child. That's all you need to know. And that you can tell by looking."

The Chieftain's Man smiled at the chatter. He measured Din's chest, his thighs together.

"Sit down," said the Chieftain's Man, and he measured Din sitting on a rock. He measured his hand span.

"What is it?" Din said. "What are you doing? Am I dead? Are you measuring me for burial?" He took up a knife and pierced his thumb. "No, look, the blood, you see. I'm not dead, I'm not sick. The only person in the village who's sick is the Chieftain and he shows no sign of recovery. Him you could be measuring for death, though I don't expect anyone would dare to do such a thing." Din gasped. The Chieftain's Man smiled at him.

"You don't mean . . . " Din could not speak.

"The Chieftain will see you after evening meal. He's at his clearest then. You wash that stench off. His nose is sensitive and likes nothing to offend it. Come naked if you can stand the cold. It won't hurt you and your clothing is beyond redemption. You may win favor instead. Perhaps one of the ladies may see otherwise hidden talents."

"There is nothing hidden. Nothing surprising," Din said. He slumped.

The Chieftain's Man slapped him on the back. "Come earlier rather than later," he said, and he left the den.

Din stepped out at dusk and walked. Chatter stopped when he came near so he was sure something was afoot. He walked on, wanting to see the horizon at sunset, sit by the aromatic patch of blooms and breathe its scent. He sat for a while, enjoying the silence, when a footfall alerted him to the approach of a large man. Din looked over his shoulder, knowing there was no danger. Even in the falling light he knew it was the Chieftain's Man.

"How is your son?" asked Din, without turning around.

The Chieftain's Man said, "My son is well." He touched Din on the shoulder. "Thank you, Din. You need to come now."

Din rose, brushing seeds from his clothes. "I haven't eaten yet," he said.

"You can eat later. Eating is not important. You will eat well later."

Din felt cold. He shivered. "Well, then, let's go before my belly forces me elsewhere," he said. He stripped naked and left his clothes in a pile.

The Chieftain's Den was smoky and reeked of blood. The Chieftain lay on a pelt-covered slab. Around him were small flames, keeping the room warm. Earthenware jars surrounded him. Din knew these contained all the Chieftain's bodily fluids and waste; nothing would spill to earth. At the time of death, all parts are collected and buried. In the corner the great hulking Brewer mixed his soup. A ladle of the Chieftain's blood. A pinch of dirt from below the ever-living tree. A smear of shit. He looked up when Din arrived and nodded. "Good," he said.

The Chieftain tried to raise his head. Din was shocked at his decline. As his fluids drained from him, he weakened.

"Good," said the Chieftain. "Raise me." The Brewer raised his head, pushing a bundle of clean cloth under his neck. The Brewer gave him something to swallow and his eyes brightened, the blood dripped more rapidly into the jars.

"Din, you are a good man," said the Chieftain. Din heard a rustling, a tearing, and there was the clothes-maker, working in the corner.

The Den was very crowded. The Brewer said, "Forgive me,"

and pulled a handful of hair from the Chieftain's head. He thrust these into the soup he was cooking then handed the wet strands to the cloth-maker. The cloth maker sewed them into the clothes.

"Do you have a family, Din?" said the Chieftain.

"My family is dead," Din said. He did not remind the Chieftain who had killed them.

The Chieftain grimaced. "Yes. So I will offer you a boon. It seems only fair." He breathed so deeply and for so long Din thought he must have fallen asleep. But then, "You will travel to the five surrounding villages. There will be a woman waiting ready for you in each village. Their Chieftains have agreed, and I have agreed for them. We may not know if you manage to make the babies, you and I. We won't know. But others will. You can make five babies to carry your name.

"This is my boon."

Din nodded. He knew there was more and these words he dreaded.

"For this boon I ask of you something very great." The Chieftain looked Din in his eyes for the first time in his life. "I have chosen you for three reasons. One, your size. Two, your hearing is good and your observation sharp, and three, your patience. I have seen you sit for hours just watching, oblivious to the world writhing about you. I could not wish for a better guard."

Din's throat constricted as if filled with dirt. "Guard?"

"Yes, Din. You will come with me into the ground and you will guard me for all eternity. As long as you protect me, your family will prosper greatly. Any lapse will mean suffering for your children's children. To fail in your task will mean a terrible death for your entire family. You must work quickly. I have only three days."

Din said, "I'm not sure I can father children."

"Your father managed, didn't he?" said the Chieftain. He lay back, closed his eyes. "Be quick, Din. Make your family."

It occurred to Din that if he refused, if he did not sire a family with whom he could be threatened, perhaps he could guard for a few years, then slip away. But the idea of fathering a dynasty was something he found enticing. To think his children would prosper over those of the Chieftain and all those who sneered. Din's name beside the Chieftain's. Din's name remembered.

He travelled by wagon to the other villages. He sipped the foul drink given to him by the Brewer, a drink usually reserved for the nights when the Chieftain was making babies. Each sip gave Din strength, and he began to think in detail about the women waiting for him.

He was not disappointed. The women had vied to bear his seed. They trusted him to guard well. They anticipated prosperity and fame. They dreamed of their great-grandchildren living in comfort and wealth. One woman he couldn't visit; when he arrived, her blood flags were hanging by her door. He was given food by the people there then he rode on.

Din tried to memorize their names and a little about them but it was difficult. The youngest one was the most voracious, the oldest timid. The most beautiful woman he had ever seen made him enter her four times to be sure.

Then there was the one he would always think of, in his seat in the tomb. She was short, masculine, her voice rough, yet he loved her voice because she spoke to him and he spoke back and she asked him his parent's names so she would know what to call their child. He did not want to leave her.

"If we leave now we may be far enough away when my Chieftain dies and they will have to choose someone else," he said.

She shook her head. "No, Din. This is our only time together. Now you have a responsibility to your unborn child, to make this the best life possible. That is what you must do."

Din said, "But we could have happy children by being happy together."

"What about our grandchildren? And great-grandchildren? What about the children ten generations from now who will not even know of our existence? And anyway, Din," she said, gazing out to the field, "What makes you think we would be happy together?"

Din closed his eyes to forget her face at that moment and he thought instead of her face as he stroked her naked back, and how she had asked him what his parent's names were.

There was loud shouting and she gathered herself together.

"Where is he?" The shouting came to Din and he realized. "Here, I'm here."

"The Chieftain needs you," said the Chieftain's Man.

The clothes prepared for Din were the softest he had ever worn. On his seat there were many soft layers, to comfort him through his years of sitting.

The Chieftain breathed harshly but did not wake. The Brewer collected the last of his blood, stirred it into the soup and said to Din, "Don't spill a drop."

Din swallowed it and it made him think of rats, how a rat would taste if you squeezed it till the juice ran. He spilled nothing on his beautiful clothes.

Around him the wailing, the weeping started. The Chieftain was still. Din stared at him.

"You should fill your eyes with something else," said the Brewer. "You will see nothing but that sight for all eternity."

Din could sense the color draining from his vision. The smell of the room faded too, the sounds were fainter. All he could hear was a fly walking over the Chieftain's face, and Din leaned forward to flick the fly away.

"Good start," said the Chieftain's Man. He led Din to his

chair, the first of Din's life. It was a perfect fit. The Chieftain was carried to his burial hole, followed by the treasures, and the jars containing the Chieftain's bodily fluids and waste, then Din, then the woman carrying Din's last meal. He wished he had eaten before the Brewer's draught, because he could feel his taste buds dying on his tongue as he was carried along.

"Keep him safe," people shouted.

"Stay awake," they said.

"Save yourself," one voice screamed, but Din couldn't turn in his chair to see.

The Chieftain was placed in the deep hole lined with wood and the greatest of materials. His things around him.

Then Din's chair was settled in a perfectly-built alcove. A sword was placed across his lap and he felt the etchings there, detailed pictures inlaid of the Chieftain's life and there, at the hilt, Din thought, was his chair and Din, sitting there with a beard grown past his feet.

"Goodbye, Din. Think of your family," said the Chieftain's Man.

The tomb was sealed off as Din ate his last meal. Feeling it sit heavy and indigestible in his belly, he could hear, very faintly, the sound of an ocean full of dirt being piled on top of him.

Time passed strangely. Din was only aware of the Chieftain, his treasures, his body slowly dissolving into muck, his bones left there to guard. Sometimes the sound of digging and he fleetingly thought of his children, his grandchildren, coming to give him absolution, to tell him they were okay and they could look after themselves. This never happened. By his alertness he guarded the burial mound from all attention and invasion.

He saw generations of insects, millennia of insects. He never slept, never moved. He did not itch and had no waste to be expelled. He did not sneeze.

And then he saw the bones stirring. He watched, thinking perhaps his eyes were tired and he should shut them for just a moment to rest them. No, he thought, there is movement. The jaw. The fingers. If Din was breathing before, he stopped now. He squeezed his eyes; that hurt. He felt it.

"Din," the Chieftain spoke. "Din, you are good. You have kept me safe." The skeleton clicked. "Din, one of you has not been vigilant. One of you has slept and let his mound be entered."

The skeleton clicked again, and a sound almost like swallowing.

"Oh, yes, there are others. Other chieftains, princes, kings, in places you can't even imagine. We all need a guard, Din. Oh, I'm lucky to have you.

"Din, you will leave here for just a moment. You will see the price paid for failure. Then you will return to guard me."

"But how?" said Din. No words but the Chieftain answered.

"You will enter the body of a descendant. You were very successful, Din. You have a very large family."

Din blinked. This wasn't painful. And then . . .

And then he breathed fresh air. The scent of it almost made him sick. He stumbled over his skirts. His skirts. He was a woman. Running. Running with so many others he was swept up.

Part of him was aware of the deathly stillness of the tomb; his body still sat unmoving. The feeling of movement in this strange body shocked him so much it was all he could think about; elbows and knees bending, eyes blinking, throat swallowing, lungs breathing. Then the dust being raised by his thumping feet, the rocks cutting into his soles.

Around him people ran, some forward, some back, falling over, shouting, confusion. Din was carried this way and that, "Beware," someone shouted to him, "Watch the baby," and he looked down for a baby on the ground, thinking to step over it and it was his own belly protruding.

"My baby," he said. The voice was that of his descendant. He couldn't tell how many generations he had spent guarding the Chieftain.

He wondered which of the mothers sent this line forward.

He tripped then, falling over an old man.

"Get off me, woman," said the old man. Blood covered his face. "Get off me, leave me alone to die." People ran about them, screaming, and Din could hear a noise, a crashing, and it was men coming, protected men with weapons. Din understood these things with the sense of his descendent.

"Come on," he said to the old man. "Stand up and come on. If we can get to the side there we can crawl under that wagon and perhaps they will run by us."

The old man shook his head. "I'm too tired." The men with weapons were killing, now, slashing their way through the citizens like they were cutting through tall, sharp grass.

"Come on," said Din. He dragged at the old man till he stood, then helped him through the crowd. Bruised, damaged, uncut, they reached the wagon. There was room underneath for them both, even with Din's huge belly. Heavy jewelry dug into Din as he crawled and he wondered at its worth. They squatted, watching feet running, falling, blood reaching in thick tendrils and threatening to soak their toes.

"They'll find us," said the old man.

"Perhaps not," said Din. He felt there was an irony here, the squashing into a dark place smelling someone else's stench. He felt a kick.

"Oh!" he said. "It must be the baby."

"Shhh," said the old man, but he reached over in the darkness and rested his hand to feel the strength of the unborn child.

They sat like that for a long time.

Then at last it quieted. The bodies were left in piles and the men went away to celebrate, to drink.

Then new feet came, unshod, tentative. They could see a person squatting by this body and that, seeking something.

"Cyrus?" said the old man softly. "Cyrus?" He crawled to the edge of the wagon and dared to peek out.

"Cyrus! Cyrus! Here!"

"Father! Father! You're alive! We have transport, we need to leave now." He paused as he saw Din.

"Yes, yes. She will be coming with us." The old man turned to Din. "You and your child will be well rewarded." He smiled. "Very well rewarded."

"Thank you," said Din. As he crawled out from under the wagon, he felt himself lifting, leaving, and he could have cried for the loss of it, the loss of feeling, and knowledge, the loss of it all.

"You see, Din?" said the skeleton. "An entire family dead, and many others beside. You must guard me with vigilance and never, ever let go. Your family is large now, and prosperous. You should be proud." This last word sighed from the lips of the skeleton so softly and for so long Din felt it like a breeze against his cheek. The breeze felt cool and Din wondered if there was any chance tears had fallen while he had been away.

There were times Din wished failure on other guards. Times he wished for momentary release just to see, to see his children and how they looked. This would mean people dying, though, a family destroyed.

Din still wished for their failure.

"Oh, Din, another one gone," the skeleton groaned. He spoke no more, though Din imagined his heart racing. Preparing to see the world.

Din grew to mistrust the words. He stayed still, and watched. Sometimes he heard scrabbling above his head and knew the mound was being explored; he opened his eyes wide and clutched his sword and the exploration stopped.

Din didn't know how it worked, only that if he noticed them they were gone.

Then the skeleton sat up again.

"Oh, Din, Din, so many gone. You are still here, though. Oh, Din, I picked well. Would you like to see how your family is doing? And watch the demise of those others? Oh, there have been so many. I've protected you from so much, Din, much I could have shown you."

Din's heart raced, he squeezed his eyes and he was lying down, lying down, and he stretched his legs for the joy of it. Stretched out and the bed was soft, the covers warm, what animal skin was it? He curled and stretched and moved his limbs because he could. The room smelt dank but not too bad and he sat up to see candles flickering around the walls.

There was a mirror in the corner and Din rose to see his face, how many generations beyond and he a young man, handsome, one scar over his eye. Din felt proud of it, a battle won.

"Baron! Baron! Step up! The battle is almost lost."

"Who is it?" shouted Din. The voice on the other side of the door said, "It's me, Baron, your servant. We are safe here but we could rise to watch the end of the battle."

"Are many dying?"

"The rider says yes. He says they will all be killed."

"Are we happy about this?" Din pulled a heavy robe over his shoulders and opened the door. His servant was there, small and red-faced. He fidgeted from foot to foot.

"They're saying the blood is running into the river and it will not clear again for many years. We could see it if we leave now."

Din knew his Chieftain wanted him to see but he did not want to waste precious moments of freedom watching others die.

"Is there anyone else here?"

"Your family is asleep, Baron. The children were frightened by your talk but they sleep now."

"I shouldn't frighten them."

"No. But they love it." Din glanced at his servant, wondering at his familiarity. His lack of servitude. He thought perhaps there was a physical likeness, that the Baron sowed his seed quite wide.

"How many children do I have?" Din wondered. "How many of us are there?" He smiled. He wondered if the woman who had asked his parents' names was the one responsible for this part of the family.

There was a great banging and the servant said, "News!" He ran to discover more. Din opened doors and peered inside until he found the children. There were eight, he thought, all of them angelic. Tears from Din.

He wanted to hold one of his children, so he climbed into the bed. His ears and toes were frozen. He climbed in and smelt the child, his child, breathed it in and that was the smell he took back with him to the tomb.

"They will all die if you fail," said the Chieftain. "Your proud line will end. You must carry on."

And time passed and Din waited and guarded and sometimes was released. Glimpses of the world as it changed and grew. The cloth on his body, so different every time, the smells, the things people used to move themselves about. The terrible things they used to kill each other with.

The skeleton crumbled until the bones lay in pieces. The gold, the treasures were safe. The voice came from the pile sometimes and to pass the time Din thought of his family, the millions of them he thought must be his.

And then he was released again, and the world was almost odorless.

It took him a moment to realize he had been released, because his body was still sitting, hands still holding something, feet still flat on the floor.

The cloth of his body felt like skin, not fur, not woven cloth like he had worn before. It moved as he moved, was soft and comfortable.

He sat before a vast window which looked out into the night. The moon shone brightly and it seemed closer to Din than it had on other visits.

Din tried to stand but found he couldn't move.

"Do you have a request?" The voice was in his head.

"I wanted to get up. To move."

There was silence.

"Where to?" said the voice.

"Just to stand," said Din. He wanted to stretch his legs.

"You can move now," said the voice, and the bar he was holding receded into the chair. He stood up. His legs felt odd. Thin and not much use.

He moved close to the window and looked out.

Din recoiled. Below him the ground was so brightly lit it hurt his eyes.

"The lights are so bright," he said. The words hurt his throat, as if his descendant had not spoken for a long time.

The lights dimmed instantly. Din stepped back to the window.

He could see himself now, his descendant reflected faintly in the window. He was pale and bald and to Din he looked weak and sick.

"Where are you?" said Din. He looked out of the window now the light didn't hurt his eyes and he could see many thousands of small gray buildings, lined up along narrow paths.

"Do you want to see me?" said the voice.

"Yes," said Din. He wanted to talk. "Where are you?"

"I'm here." Din turned to the voice, not in his head now. A pale, bald, beautiful woman stood before him.

"What is it you need?"

"I want to see out there. What's out there?"

"The people. It's the people," she said.

"They live in those small mounds?"

She looked puzzled. "What is this about?" she said. "What is your concern?"

"I need to see them," Din said. He started to panic. The smell of the tomb was returning and he knew his time was almost up.

"They're okay. It's the others you should worry about." The woman led Din to a screen. There were pictures there, not a war but people dying. Their mouths yawned at Din.

"The illness," said the woman. "It's not safe outside."

"But I'd like to see what it's like out there." He gestured to the small buildings below.

The woman shrugged. "Sit down."

She touched his arm as he settled himself and he saw it, the confines, the fake light, the food provided so bland, the work so dull. *Is this it?* thought Din. *Death or this?* He choked. The room dimmed and he was back in the tomb, doing his duty.

"You see, Din? You see what happens to those who fail?" and Din couldn't breathe he was so tired and he closed his eyes, just closed them, and he heard the skeleton whining, and he let his hands fall, he heard digging above and he wondered as he fell asleep who could be left to desecrate the grave he had guarded for all of his eternity.

GUARDING THE MOUND: A COMMENTARY

VERY FEW WRITERS CAN PULL OFF A STORY THAT spans eternity, but somehow Kaaron Warren makes it happen in this cleverly constructed tale that puts us in the position of a Chieftain's guard in the afterlife.

What makes Warren's story so intriguing is that it establishes Din's narrative as a kind of "coming of age" story that equates adulthood with a doomed fate. It begins with Din's envy of adulthood among the hunters of his tribe, a teenage desire for autonomy that all readers can identify with, but when he goes off on his own to prove himself he becomes locked into a role for a competing tribe that robs him of his tribal identity and fixes him into a permanent alienation. As a graveyard guard, he is cast into a role that is essentially powerless across time, despite the physical power implied by his function as a guardian. The tribe he protects is essentially a metaphor for patriarchy, as the boy becomes a man only by protecting the male ruler... and the changes that happen in the world over time here are a sobering lesson in what this kind of masculinist social structure might lead to.

—Michael Arnzen, PhD

BORN AND BREAD

THERE WAS ONCE A BABY BORN SO UGLY HER father packed his bags in fury when he saw her.

"Who did you lie with, the baker or his dough?" he called over his shoulder as he left. Already he was planning to surprise his girlfriend who always smiled when she saw him and asked for nothing.

"Only you!" her mother called back. She held the baby in a soft brown blanket, though she had to lean against the wall for support.

The baby was as heavy as a calf and the size of the award-winning pumpkin at the fair five years earlier, a pumpkin that had never been matched before or since. Yet the baby had slid out sweetly, like dough through a piping bag.

And yes, she was pale, pasty, and fleshy.

"Don't leave her in the sun," Mrs. Crouch, the cruelest woman in the village said. "Or you'll have a loaf of bread for a daughter." (In her defense, her husband spat brown juice wherever he stood, beat her with a stick when he felt inclined, terrified the children with ghost tales, and never, ever spent a dollar when a cent would do.)

Still, the mother loved the daughter very much, especially once she learned how to laugh. Chuckles bubbled out of her like the froth in fermenting yeast, and anybody close by couldn't help but join in. She was so gentle and sweet they called her Doe, and that suited the way she had grown to look as well, like risen dough waiting to be baked into bread or sweet rolls.

Children loved to make her laugh, because her whole body quivered with it and it was beautiful to watch.

Each night she and her mother would sit together and tell stories and jokes. Sometimes her father would visit (always at dinner time. Her mother was the most marvelous cook. Her pastry was like flakes of pure heaven) and he would tell them stories of his journeys. His girlfriend was long-since departed, and he travelled the world selling and buying clever items for the kitchen. He bought Doe's mother a gadget for lemons and one for eggs, he bought spices and seasonings that made the whole house smell delicious.

Neither of them hated him for his early desertion; he was, for the most part, a good man and they loved his stories and gifts.

Each night Doe's mother would stroke, mold, press, and kneed her flesh, stretch and smooth it. Sometimes this hurt, but it also always felt good.

By the time Doe was eighteen, she had transformed into a beautiful, lithe young woman with a sense of humor, an infectious laugh, and a vast storehouse of stories.

In short, she became marriageable.

She had no interest in such a thing, though. She knew she could not have children because those parts of her were not fully formed and she saw no other reason to tie herself to one man.

Like her father, she enjoyed journeys, explorations, and with her mother's blessings and warnings, her father's financial help, she set out for adventure.

She spent ten years exploring the world, tasting, seeing, learning, becoming, loving. She ate damper, dinkelbrot, pain de mie, bagels, sangak, roti, and pandesal. She learned how to cook each loaf, loved to watch it brown, hug it to her chest warm from the oven. And like each loaf, each lover felt different, because she could mold herself around them. Encase them. More than once a man wept after their lovemaking.

"Nothing. Ever. So beautiful." The words in gasps.

Each encounter left her dented and stretched. She could massage herself back into shape, but she missed her mother's gentle touch and the stories they shared.

One day, her mother contacted her. "Your father is buying me a wonderful gift. A bakery! I will make cakes people will want to keep forever and others they will eat while still standing at the shop counter and order another."

"Will you bake bread?" Doe asked

"If you come back, you can be the bread baker. My dear little Doe."

But Doe had changed. She felt as if all she'd eaten, smelt, and seen so much; all the men she'd loved, all the women she'd spoken with, all the stories and jokes she'd shared: all of this had altered her. Would her mother still love her?

Her mother sighed as they embraced, but there was no judgment, no disappointment. "I've missed you!" she said, and her fingers pressed and stroked until Doe felt ordinary again.

And she set to work baking the most wonderful breads for her mother's bakery.

All this is to explain how it could be that Doe helped to fulfill the awful Mr. Crouch's dying wishes and thus lay his cruel ghost to rest.

As he lay on his deathbed he said to Mrs. Crouch, "You have been a bad wife. Only this many times have we had relations." There is some dissention as to how many fingers he held up. "You owe me three more. After my death, you will lie with me three nights, or this village will suffer the consequences."

He lay back, then, and demanded bread. He loved Doe's tiger bread and chose that as his last meal.

Doe walked into his sick room. Even though she'd been warned, the stench was overwhelming. She knew the odor of yeast left to ferment too long, but that was nothing compared to this. She'd smelt dead animals in the roof drains and the worst toilets any nightmare could dredge up. She'd smelt a man who hadn't bathed for twenty years.

Nothing came close to the stench of this room.

She pinched her nose and squeezed to close her nostrils.

"Here she is, the beautiful baker," Mr. Crouch said. "Come and knead me, darling. I am ready for you," and he weakly tugged away the covers to reveal his naked body.

She placed the tray of bread beside him and left the room.

It's said he choked on a crust; that was not Doe's doing.

They buried him three nights later. The women in town went to Mrs. Crouch, to help prepare her to go to his grave.

She said, "He was repulsive alive. I cannot lie with him dead. And you know he was a cruel man; he means to damage me. Destroy me."

She refused go that first night, and the next day ten fields were found withered.

She refused to go that second night, and the next day the clinic for the unwell was burnt down. Many would have been lost were it not for the early-rising Doe and her mother, who sounded the alarm.

The villagers went to Mrs. Crouch to beg her to lie with her dead husband. "He will take the children next. You know he will," they said.

She refused. "He means to destroy me. Mar me for life, haunt me into eternity, kill me."

They turned from her, distraught but not surprised. She was

selfish and cruel and didn't care about the rest of them.

"I am driven by bad fortune! All my life!" she called after them, as if that made a difference.

Doe had led a blessed life, really. Full of good fortune and windfalls.

She went to Mrs. Crouch, who sneered at her as she always did.

"My deepest sympathies," Doe said, and she held Mrs. Crouch close, squeezing until she made an imprint in Doe's soft body.

In the bakery, she mixed dough, let it rise, punched it down, shaped it, let it rise again.

She baked this bread hard and brown. She baked Mrs. Crouch with her eyes closed.

As the moon rose high, she carried the bread lady to the cemetery. It was light, as good bread should be.

She laid it on Mr. Crouch's grave. "Darling," she called out. "Darling, I'm here."

Then she tripped away to hide.

At first, there was stillness, a terrible quiet that made her doubt her ears. Then a disturbance in the dirt, a writhing, then four nubs appeared, then eight, like pink growing tendrils of an unpleasant plant.

He rose up naked and fully erect.

He fell upon his bread lady, roaring, biting, thrusting, filled with lust and fury. Doe looked away and she thought, *I will tell her I understand. What woman could lie with this man and ever feel clean again?*

He fell upon his dough-wife, the Lady Bread, and his sweat, his juice, the dampness of the air, helped to dissolve the bread into a pale mush. He did not seem to care. He stood up, shook himself like a dog, then nodded and sank into his grave.

All at once sound returned; the rustling leaves, the howling dogs, and Doe felt that she could leave.

In the morning, the only tragedy found was Mrs. Crouch, strangled with her own hands clenched around her neck, her eyes wide, tears dried in a map across both cheeks.

There was reward to be had though.

On clearing the Crouch's house, their fortune was found, and this shared amongst them all. Not only that, but for a dozen years to come the crops grew tall and golden and brought good fortune to them all.

As for Doe . . . as her mother aged, they looked for a baker to take her place. One day he came to them, and Doe felt soft on the inside as she had never felt before.

His hands were warm and she could feel her flesh shift at his touch. He could mold dough like an artist and needed only four hours sleep a night.

All the village was happy for their Doe.

And that is all to explain why, each year on December the 21st, the villagers all buy the perfect Lady Bread, thus bringing good luck upon themselves and upon the village and all who pass through her.

BORN AND BREAD: A COMMENTARY

FANTASY FICTION OFTEN USES PERSONIFICATION, metaphor, and allegory to tell us about ourselves through an alternative lens. In "Born and Bread," which draws from a Russian fairy tale ("Sivka Burka"), we get an exemplary example of an extended metaphor: the body of the lead character named Doe is treated literally as if she were made of *dough*.

Rife with wordplay and allusions to baking and bread, this rich flash fiction piece is virtually a prose-poem dedicated not merely to the body, but to the *female* body. When Doe comes of age and becomes "marriageable" she explores the world of breads—i.e. her sexuality—achieving a kind of mastery over them, and herself. She returns home as a baker, educated in the power and potential of her body and the ways of love.

The story does not focus merely on Doe's becoming a woman, *per se*, but on how she puts her knowledge about love to work by saving her hometown from a ghoul by fooling him into raping a kind of straw man—a false "Lady Bread"—that puts his otherworldly lust to final rest and raises her status to hero. Thereafter, her bread becomes a kind of communion wafer, bonding the community in a new ritual—not over the body of a Jesus figure who dies for their sins, but over a death to the sin of sexual objectification itself.

—Michael Arnzen, PhD

Death's Door Café

THEO THOUGHT OF THE PAIN IN HIS VEINS AS THE clawing of bats, the smell in his nose their guano, the rawness of his throat torn by their smoke. It was this, the pain in breathing, that made him climb out of his car at last and walk a block to the Dusseldorf Café.

The large purple door had a suburban brass knocker and a spy hole. A plaque beside the door read *The Soldier*. In larger text: b1922, d1946.

Up close, he could see dark stains in the wood. He touched his fingers to the marks, feeling the door's thick grain, wondering if he'd get a sense of "ending," an understanding of the death it had once concealed.

He knocked.

When the waiter opened the door, Theo jumped back. He turned away, wanting to run, knowing he wasn't able. Once, he could have been around the corner before the waiter even raised a hand. Now . . . he had no choice. Even walking one block from the car had sapped his strength.

"Table for one?" said the waiter. "Did you have a booking?"

Theo shook his head. The café wasn't in the phonebook or online; he'd only found it by walking up and down the street.

"That'll be okay, we can squeeze you in. A cancellation, aren't you lucky?"

Theo stepped inside. The waiter led Theo across the room,

saying, "There's a great table over here in the corner. Right next to the magazines." Theo stood close to him.

"Who was The Soldier? If that's not a rude question."

"It's always the first thing people want to know: Who died behind the door?" The waiter's face shifted, became serious. "The Soldier was back from war a year, and he was listening to some gloomy music, some sad sort of song, they say, when there was a knock on that door." The waiter rapped loudly on the table and Theo jumped.

The waiter handed him the menu.

Theo hadn't eaten solid food for more than a week. Even glancing at the Chef's Specialties list, with its "South Coast Swordfish" and its "Hazelnut Chocolate Soufflé," made him feel ill.

"The super special today is a lamb tagine with blood plums. The chef tells me it's very good," the waiter said. "So the soldier opens the door, that very door you came through, and who is standing there but his old sergeant? And the sergeant says, 'You've brought shame to an entire division,' and he reaches in and slashes the soldier's throat. The soldier bleeds to death so fast, he's gone by the time the killer reaches the front gate. They say the music was still playing two days later when the body was found. As if that poor dead soldier kept hitting replay." The waiter shrugged. "So, what'll it be?"

Theo felt sick. "Could I just have a green salad?" he said. The waiter smiled.

"We sell a lot of green salads. Chef does a very good one. Anything else for now? Some nice toast? We sell a lot of toast, too."

Theo nodded. Smiled. His dry lips cracked. He didn't know what to say, how to ask for what he wanted.

"Drinks?"

Theo shook his head. "I'm not really drinking. I'm..." He

hadn't told anyone yet, and he didn't know what words to use. "I'm not well."

"Oh, you poor thing. How about I bring you one of our fabulous Virgin Marys? We leave out the vodka for sick people." The waiter smiled. "We get a lot of your type in here."

The café was full, but remarkably quiet. Gentle music played, something with pan pipes and an ethereal female voice. The chair was comfortable; high-backed, soft-seated. Theo shifted back to give himself more room and there was no scraping sound, as if the legs were muffled. The walls were painted all around with a mural he took to depict Dusseldorf and the River Rhine. Along the banks, stylish people strolled, perfectly groomed, laughing, small dogs at their feet.

There was nothing dark, no hint of death beyond the door he had walked through.

Theo couldn't eat his green salad when it arrived, but he drank his tomato juice. He watched to see what people did. He wanted a clue, didn't want to mess up, miss out.

An emaciated woman held a bread stick. She was dressed in hot pink as if to draw attention away from her pale face. Her companion, a red-cheeked woman with a high, far-reaching voice, did all the talking, frivolous stuff. She barely took a breath. Theo thought she was frightened the sick woman would speak. He understood this kind of avoidance.

He had good hearing (*Batboy*, his mother called him, because he picked up everything) and didn't have to strain to listen in.

"They've got it in green, blue, brown, orange and red," the healthy woman said. "But they don't have all the sizes, you'd have to try them on to see. But first you'd decide if you wanted green, blue, brown, orange or red. I, me, I'd choose red or orange though I wouldn't mind brown . . . " without a break, desperately filling each space.

Finally the sick woman reached out a finger and touched the loud woman's wrist. The loud woman stopped instantly.

The sick woman nodded.

"Waiter! Waiter. We're ready to see Jason now," the loud woman said, waving the menu.

Theo opened his menu. The owner's name was there, in large, ornate type. "Your host, Jason Davies," it said.

Jason Davies came and sat at the table with the women. He was young, black hair, pale blue eyes. Theo saw the patrons in the room all watching him. Nobody spoke or moved; all focused on him.

He talked with the sick woman for a while (*"How did you hear about us? And is this a friend? A relative?" "I've answered all this,"* she said. *"I've told you."*) then led her through a door at the back of the café. She walked slowly, relying heavily on a cane.

Theo swallowed. Winced.

The friend stood by their table, clutching her handbag. She started toward the back door, but the waiter gently led her to walk toward the front.

"Leave it with us, now."

"I need to give her a lift home. She can't manage."

He smiled. "She'll be fine."

He moved over to Theo. "Can we help you with anything else today, or just the bill?"

"Could I see the owner? Jason? Can I talk to Jason?" he asked, wondering if he was being reckless, ruining his chances. The waiter stood by the table and looked at him.

"Come back tomorrow."

"I can't. I haven't got the time," and that meant a different thing to someone with cancer.

"I'll ask him," the waiter said. "You may have to wait. What's your name?"

It was fifteen minutes before the waiter said, "He can't see you today. Maybe next time."

"How many visits until you're considered worthy?" Theo asked. He hoped he didn't sound sarcastic. He meant the question.

"It's not so much worthiness. Often it's persistence."

"How many times did that woman visit?"

"I'm not sure. Many. Many times. Some of our regulars come for months."

"But I may not have months."

The waiter looked at him.

"Jason will know."

Theo felt a ticking in his ears, sign that waves of pain were on their way. He paid. The waiter said, "Come back soon. Tomorrow's special is French Onion Soup. It's fantastic. If I had to choose a last meal, that would be it."

His direct gaze told Theo, *I'm not joking and I'm not being cruel.*

He handed Theo a sheet of paper. *Questionnaire*, it said. "Bring it with you next time," the waiter said, ushering Theo out. "Be as honest as you can. That's what Jason always says."

In the car, Theo swallowed pain killers and waited for the nausea to pass before driving. His doctor had told him he shouldn't be on the road, but that was advice he would ignore for as long as possible.

He looked at the twenty-page questionnaire. *What do you fear, what do you love, what do you miss most about childhood, where do you think you are going to, do you believe in God? Are you ever tongue-tied or lost for words? What will you do with the rest of your life?* He laughed; he hadn't answered such personal questions since a long-ago girlfriend had wanted to know everything about him before making a real commitment.

That hadn't worked out so well.

Before he was five pages in, he was tired. He listened to podcasts: stuff about good eating habits, slow cooking, a bat cave near Denpasar Town, Bali where the bats are known to keep bad things at bay, and children's theatre. He watched people come and go from the café, so many of them clearly ill. He liked watching them.

Two hours passed.

He had nowhere to go.

Three hours.

Then he saw the woman all in pink. She must have left via the back door. She seemed taller and she had no cane. She put out her hand for a taxi, then lowered her arm and walked to a bus stop. As Theo watched, she counted the money she held. Shook her head. Laughed.

He started the car, drove alongside her and offered her a lift. "I was in the café," he said. "Death's Door Café."

"You were? I'm sorry. I noticed very little."

In the café, she had looked over fifty. Now, she seemed to be in her mid-thirties. Her face glowed, and she bounced on her feet as if full of energy.

She leant into his car. Looked at him. Then climbed in.

"Where do you want me to drop you?'

She seemed a bit stunned by this. Lost for words. "To your friend's house?"

"No! No. To the airport. I'm, *ahhh* ... "

"Holiday?"

"Holiday." She looked at the money in her hand again.

"You need money."

She shook her head. Then nodded. She laughed. "I'm not sure, actually."

Theo smiled. "I can buy you a ticket. Easy. Money's just burning a hole in my pocket."

"What would you want in return?"

"Nothing, really. Just to talk."

"I can't tell you anything,"

"You look fantastic."

"I do, don't I? And I feel better than I have in maybe two decades."

"So what happened in there?"

"I can't say. I really can't. Not even for a plane ticket."

"I'm going to buy you that anyway," he said. It really did mean nothing to him. Even ten thousand dollars wouldn't make a dent. "But . . . how do I get in? How do I get Jason to talk to me?"

They approached the airport.

He said, "Do you want me to give a message to your friend?"

She stared at him for a moment. "Oh. No. No. Best not. Look, if you want to get in? Keep going back. And be honest. As honest as you can force yourself to be. And good luck."

She kissed his cheek, her lips warm, soft, alive.

"Keep going back," she said.

Theo was not the only regular.

Some had a constant companion, like the little boy and his mother. She carried him in, set him up with pillows. Ordered a milkshake, chocolate cake, but that made the boy cry with frustration. He took a sip, but Theo could see that it rose straight away back into his mouth.

They were invited through the door on the day the boy didn't stir as the mother walked in with him.

Some were always alone. These, like Theo, carried a book or magazine to read, or concentrated on phones, not wanting to look lonely or needy. They exchanged glances, sometimes sat together, but they didn't talk. Theo wondered if amongst them were potential friends, or long-term partners. The mother of his child. But all they really had in common was illness.

Some came in with a new companion every time, paid

nurses. An elderly man who walked with a cane always had his nurse bring gifts; he owned a series of stores, Theo discovered. He never said anything, just smiled as the nurse handed out pens, notebooks, chocolates.

A sort of camaraderie built amongst them. There were light cheers any time one was allowed through to the back.

Jason Davies sometimes nodded at them. Sometimes he'd smile. The regulars would exchange looks when one of them was so blessed.

Day after day, Theo drank carrot and ginger juice, ate dried yam chips. At times, the nausea would be too much and he would push through the beaded doorway, (*Mountain Walker*, the plaque beside it said, b1933, d1972), walking along the increasingly chilly hallway, open the dented back door (*Teen Singer* b1985, d2001), stumble every time over the rock which sat too close to the path, and enter the toilet, (*Three Year Old* b1998, d2001) which shared space with a laundry tub and what appeared to be rejected artwork from a teenage girl's bedroom.

He pretended to work at a variety of tables, taking his laptop in, using his phone. He spoke if spoken to, like the day when the elderly man sat at the next table, sitting with his eyes closed, humming softly. His nurse fussed over him, smiled around the room, stayed connected.

"You're a busy, busy man," she said to Theo. She was in her twenties and smelt faintly of cigarette smoke and breath mints. "What is it you do, busy all the time?"

"I've got a sonar equipment company." He handed her his business card.

"Love the bat," she said. Theo had drawn it himself; he had drawn bats from the age of five. "I love bats."

Theo was called Batman at school, because of the cave on his property. He didn't mind at all; he'd take kids there in groups, let them throw bat poo at each other, tell them things they didn't know.

After all the bats were killed, though, he couldn't bear to hear the name spoken. Each time was like a punch to the heart. He knew he deserved it, every hard hit, for not stopping the slaughter.

He didn't tell the nurse any of this. He might, he thought, if something happened between them. If she really loved bats, he could show her the cave, they could see it together and she'd cry with him, maybe.

But she didn't come again. Next time, the nurse was a man, bright faced and cheery, who made them all laugh.

One morning, Jason appeared. There was silence as always. He surveyed the room. "Can you stay for a while, Theo? It would be good to have a chat."

Theo nodded.

"Excellent," Jason said. He walked over to the elderly man, placed his hand on the back of the chair, and leaned over to whisper in his ear.

The elderly man gave a little shudder. "Me?" Theo heard him say.

Jason led the elderly man though the door. The waiter (there were three of them, Theo knew, all kind, efficient, professional) said to the nurse, "You're all done now. You'll be paid for the month. And thanks."

The other regulars congratulated Theo. He still didn't know what he was lucky about. No one discussed it. But it was a cure; they'd seen it. They knew it worked. Theo himself had seen six people go through the door and never return to the café. He'd seen three of them later, walking down the street, transformed. Flowers appeared in the café, with notes saying THANK YOU. Like flowers sent to nurses in hospital.

There was no follow-up because he knew no names, but still, even to have one day feeling that way would make it worthwhile. Even if it was just that one day.

Theo ordered herbal coffee and cheese but could swallow nothing. Sometimes he felt so exhausted, so suddenly and completely drained, he wanted to lay his head on the table and sleep. Sometimes he did nod off, wake to find himself still there, his coffee cold in front of him.

Theo was grateful for the pile of magazines, so he could withdraw into himself, not engage. Many were tourist magazines from Dusseldorf and he flicked through these, looking for things to talk about

When Jason sat down an hour later, Theo said, "How long did you live in Dusseldorf?" thinking it a safe, intelligent question.

"Never even been. I just like the sound of the name. Don't you?"

"Except people don't call your café that, do they?"

"Don't they?"

"They call it Death's Door Café."

"Because of the doors."

He pointed at the huge wooden door where the ill people entered. The door Theo wanted to enter.

"We call that Gladiator. We dunno how many died behind it. But plenty. You can see sweat marks from their hands as they stood leaning against it. Some came through okay. But plenty died."

"I'm . . . curious to know what's behind that door." Theo wished he had a script, but everyone spoke to Jason differently. "You've taken a lot of people through."

"I have. When I get to know someone well, sometimes I'll let them through."

"I'd like that. I need that."

"People do."

"But I've been given . . ." Theo couldn't say the words aloud. He'd told no one the timing, barely acknowledged to himself that his life could be counted in months.

"You like it here, don't you?"

"I do. Really. There's something very calming about the place."

"That's what we aim for. Our customers . . . mostly they've made a decision. Come to an acceptance, or had a realization. It calms you, to be in that state of mind."

Jason Davies put his hands on Theo's.

"Can you tell me who recommended you?"

"Nobody. I just heard about it."

"Usually we only accept recommendations. How did you hear about us?"

Theo blinked. "I'm afraid I eavesdropped on a plane. I guess they thought no one could hear, because they were talking under a blanket, but my hearing is very good. I had to find the place myself, though."

He knew everyone was listening, because he had heard all the other interviews, both the successes and the failures. He hadn't identified why some failed.

"Tell me about yourself," Jason said. He had the questionnaire on the table before him. "It says here your greatest fear is bats."

"No! Not at all. The death of bats. That's my greatest fear."

Jason tapped his nose. "Is this an element of your disease?"

Theo felt his cheeks flush. He rubbed his nose. All his life, blood had drained from it when he was nervous, scared or tired. Children weren't smart enough to think of connecting it to bat's white nose fungus, but he thought of it himself and he didn't mind. He liked the similarity.

"No, this is just nerves. My fingertips go white sometimes, too. It's not life-threatening. Not like the bat disease. It gets carried from one cave to another by people who love bats and want to see them all. One of those ironies."

"People are a bit like that, aren't they?"

He asked Theo about bats, simple questions, leading him to feel comfortable, relaxed.

"All right. Look, come through."

Jason led the way through the gladiator door, through a short hallway to a bright-red door covered with stickers of unicorns, rainbows and puppies. *Family of four* b1952, b1953, b1975, b1980, d1984. Theo touched it.

"Father gathered them in the toy room and shot them all," said Jason. "Incredible tragedy. But don't things lose their awfulness over time? Become gossip, or matters of curiosity?"

Theo realized he was asking an actual question.

"It's still awful, isn't it? That the children died. And the wife." Theo thought he heard voices inside and the sound of a ball bouncing.

Jason smiled. "Yes. Of course it is. What doesn't kill you makes you stronger."

Theo thought this made no sense at all.

Jason led Theo to a small, sunny alcove. A young woman sat there, sipping from a delicate tea cup. Her black hair was soft around her head.

"This is Cameron. She's going to ask you some questions, talk to you a bit about your questionnaire."

Theo sat down and smiled at Cameron. She smiled back.

"Would you like a cup of herbal tea?"

"No, thank you. I just finished one." Theo found it hard to contain his nerves, to maintain politeness.

"Okay then." She was very still and Theo was still with her. "What did you think of the questionnaire?"

He laughed. "It was pretty full on. I don't think I've ever thought about myself like that before."

Do you think of yourself as a good person? Is there anything that makes you feel guilty? How much do you give to charity each year? How many hours of voluntary work do you do each week? Do you feel guilty about the number of hours you do?

"I wasn't sure what the point was."

"The point is never meant to be clear in these things. We just want an understanding of you and your motivations. It's really an important part of the process. And, to be honest, we're not interested in helping psychopaths."

"I hope I'm not one of those."

She smiled. "You are not."

They talked for another hour. Theo hadn't felt so relaxed in a long time, and he hadn't ever talked about himself for so long. She seemed to understand about the bats, and didn't blame him for his state of loneliness. She spun her wedding ring periodically and he appreciated the signal; *this is all it is*, she was telling him. He liked things to be clear.

Jason joined them. "Feeling okay?"

Theo nodded. He didn't want to mention how he felt physically.

"Okay. So what we're talking about here is a second chance. You came to us, like all the others did, because you're desperate. You want to have another go at it. And you're tired of the pain, and the fear. Is that about right?"

"Yes." Theo's throat constricted and the word came out as a whisper.

"All right then. We need to sort out the paperwork." Jason opened the folder he carried and removed papers and a pen. "It will cost your life savings. I need to start with that. You need to begin this process with nothing to your name."

Theo had been prepared for a high price. "If I die I'll have nothing anyway."

"Exactly. That's all in the details. But then you will have to reconsider how you live your life. How you re-live it."

"What does everyone else do, given a second chance?" He wanted that as well.

"Everybody is different. Every single person."

Jason filled in the forms. Theo signed. He agreed never to kill, never to rape or maim. He agreed to live a good life, to make the most of his second chance. He signed the paper believing fully in this commitment.

"So . . . what is going to happen? Can I ask? What is the actual process?"

"We can talk about that tomorrow when you come back for your appointment."

"Come here? So is there a clinic here or something?"

"We can talk about that tomorrow." Jason said. "My suggestion is that you spend the day somewhere you care about. Somewhere important. Some will spend it with loved ones, but many prefer not to. There is nothing certain in this world and this is no exception."

Theo knew there were questions he could ask.

"It will take all you've got. We've discussed the money. But the life. You will be leaving your past behind. The people, the places. You won't want to visit your bat cave again."

"There are other bat caves."

"You'll feel nothing for them. That memory will be lessened, so much so that you will wonder where you read about it, if you think of it at all."

"I didn't know that."

"Make your visits. And decide. It's never too late to change your mind. But this may be your last chance."

Theo went to the bat cave, his first visit in seventeen months. Only the memory of them remained, but that memory was strong.

Hours spent on a rough mat on the cave floor, his face covered, listening to them, feeling the flap of their wings. Close to half a million bats was the estimation, and through three generations of Theo's family there had been no harm, no damage. Then reports came in of the diseases they carried, and one scientist was bitten. Theo couldn't even remember now if the man had died; certainly there was a lot of fuss. Theo never believed it was the bats.

His father was determined. "Too many kids here to risk," he said, because there were cousins as well as siblings, all of them working on the farm, balancing it with school.

He was advised that fire was the best, the kindest way. That the smoke would put the bats to sleep and the fire would then burn the bodies so they weren't left with half a million corpses, just a pile of ash that could be swept away.

Theo's father made the children stay in the house, but it was an old place with gaps so the smell came through dead clear. They watched smoke billowing out, saw Theo's dad dashing out for air then back in again, and again, the whole thing taking most of the day. Theo's grandfather helped, and the brothers, all Theo's uncles, no women allowed to kill. Women inside keeping the kids quiet, baking up scones and cakes, stirring soup, all of them talking bright and cheerful as if a massacre was not taking place.

Theo never forgave them for that.

It wasn't as if the advice was right; the smoke did not kill them all, so many were burnt to death. And the fire did not burn them all to ash; the bodies piled at the entrance to the cave so that Theo and his cousins had to help dig the men out. Those bat bodies still warm, some charred, and the flutter of them, the sense they were still alive when they weren't. And the smell; he'd thought he was used to guano, that he actually liked it, but this was like poison.

Years later, a journalist came to confront his father with evidence the bats hadn't needed to die.

Theo's father cried as the journalist continued relentlessly to tell him ... *you didn't have to. Those bats had lived in the cave for 150 years and you killed them.*

Theo cried, too. He said to his father, as he had said many times, "You should have saved the bats."

The farm was no longer in his family. His father was too sick to look after anything at all. His mother long gone. "Those bats. All that bat shit," his father said, coughing, furious.

The new owners didn't mind Theo visiting, as long has he didn't come knocking on the door for water. The bat cave was empty. Theo could see his own footprints in the dirt floor, and the broom marks from the last time he'd tidied up. Guano still decorated the walls and the rocks, and the smell of smoke, and the walls were dark from the fire. He lay on the ground and tried to imagine them back again, alive, generations of them coming and going and his family with no guilt on their heads.

It was there he decided. Imagine not caring anymore. Imagine not carrying this guilt, this sorrow. And this pain.

Theo couldn't eat or sleep that night. In the morning, he dressed carefully. A casual suit, a fresh, pale mauve cotton shirt, clean shoes, underwear he wasn't embarrassed by. Clothes he'd be happy to be buried in, if it came to that.

He felt as if the atmosphere at the Dusseldorf Café was charged, as if they were all watching him with envy.

The waiter brought him a carrot juice he didn't order. "On the house!" patting him on the back as if congratulating him.

Just the smell of it made Theo feel sick. He'd never been so nervous, so terrified, in all his life.

Jason came to his table after half an hour. "Come on through," he said. The other regulars all held their breath, it seemed to Theo.

As if they could bring the magic to themselves by not breathing. He wiggled his fingers goodbye.

They walked through the gladiator door.

Jason said, "Did you manage to see anyone yesterday?"

"There's not really anyone I wanted to see. My family . . . we're not really in touch. Nothing in common."

Jason nodded, smiled, as if this was ordinary, something he heard all the time. "It's the people left behind who suffer when someone dies, so a loner leaves less grief than a father of three."

"But I'm still worthy. That's part of why I'm here," said Theo. "I want time to make a family of my own, one I choose and have a chance to mold."

"Most people don't like being molded."

"I want a second chance, to make people care." Theo thought for a moment, then amended it to, "To find someone to care for. I don't want to die alone. This will give me the chance, it'll help me to find someone. It'll be different this time."

"How different?"

"I've made my money. I won't have to focus on that."

"You won't have much, though. Financially, it'll be like starting again."

"But I don't care now. I've done that. I want something else."

Jason touched his shoulder. "Good. That's very good. Now, the last thing we need to do is to get you to hand-write a letter. To cover us. It's a farewell letter of sorts."

"Who do I make it out to?"

"It needs to be to someone who knows you very well as you are now. You really have no one?"

Theo thought of his managers, his staff. "I've got people." He made it out to his vice-president.

He had little to say; he'd long since dealt with the business side of things, anticipating his own death.

"And then there's this." It was a promise of complete secrecy.

"Do not tell others what happens. You may, if you are absolutely certain they are suitable, recommend someone, but do not bring them in yourself."

They walked.

They passed through a bullet-scarred door to a long hallway. "One of Ben Hall's gang died in front of this door. Shot to death." Jason poked a finger through one of the holes.

"There is a bat cave where that gang holed up," Theo said. "No one really knows where. Or they do but they want to protect the bats."

"So many connections," Jason said. "Now, what we have back here is a series of rooms. We're going to have a look at them, and you'll choose the one which suits you."

"How will I know?"

"You'll feel an empathy. Feel it physically, almost as if you could pick it up. One of these rooms will resonate with you. You'll feel a grieving, a sense of loss. One of these rooms will make your heart beat faster, or bring a lump to your throat. You don't need to know why; you need to listen to your body."

The door on Room One looked like it had come from a ship. Inside was a small children's room.

"A child died behind this door. It was so airtight and heavy, when the ship sunk he couldn't get out. He suffocated."

"Oh, God." Theo closed his eyes. He thought he sensed movement which made him dizzy. He reached out to balance himself on Jason.

"Let's look at the others before you make up your mind."

They walked. "What's . . . actually going to happen in the room?" Theo asked. "Once I've chosen it?"

"There will be some relaxation exercises. We always start with that."

Theo thought, *I'm an idiot. No one knows I'm here. Who knows what the fuck these people are doing. I'm insane. I should go.*

"Everyone feels nervous at this point, but I don't like to pre-discuss too much. It's better this way. Tell me about what you might do with your second chance. Your questionnaire wasn't big on helping others, Theo. Would you address that, perhaps?"

"I would," Theo said. "Because it makes sense." He wasn't sure that was true.

"You might be asked to do more good than you have done before. The universe may ask this, I mean."

Theo was silent. No one had expected him to do good before. "Of course," he said. "Whatever it takes." He had an absolute terror of death, after his experience with the bats, and with his mother's passing. He wanted to avoid it for as long as possible; until he was deep in dementia and didn't notice his own dying, if possible.

The door on Room Two was narrow, with inlaid wood. It seemed Asian in influence.

"This is a popular one. Behind this door a Chinese prostitute was beaten to death over a hundred years ago." Theo leaned toward the door, wanting to touch the detail.

"This one?" Jason asked. He pushed the door open. The smell was overwhelming; incense, and perfume, as if both were present in living form.

Theo shook his head.

Room Three was a toilet with an opaque glass door.

"He died in the toilet. Fat and lazy. Heart attack at 42, lay on the floor, paralyzed, blocking the door. They couldn't get him out for four hours. Everything in the rooms is recreated precisely."

Theo shuddered. Stepped away. Put his hand over his face.

"Not that one, then. People do choose it, you'd be surprised. Smell and all."

The door to Room Four was a studded, shiny one.

"He slept through the hotel fire alarm and died of smoke inhalation. No one realized he wasn't safe."

Jason looked at Theo.

"This one could be for you."

He opened the door and they stepped inside. It was a typical, dull hotel room. The fan overhead spun slowly, slightly off kilter, and there was a sound to it like flapping bat wings.

Theo felt his throat constrict, his veins swell. He could hear them; the bats calling out, as they did when he was a child. Calling out to him, making him feel as if he belonged amongst them.

"It sounds like bats flying. Can you hear it?"

"Everybody hears something different. We all see the same thing, though."

On the bed; it looked like a man, but there was no substance to him.

"We all see it," Jason said, comforting him.

The ghost on the bed shifted onto his side. His shirt tail hung out; it was crinkled.

"What I'm going to do now is to help you into a state of deep sleep. This will help us assess your physicality, now that we understand your mentality. It'll be comfortable, and you'll wake up with a sense of calm."

Theo felt a moment of panic. He looked for cameras, for some evidence that this was weird and wrong.

"Theo, really. It's okay. You've seen the others; you know it's okay. You really, absolutely know that. Let go of your fear and allow it to happen."

Theo closed his eyes. He thought he could hear the calling of the bats, but he often did. It was a memory. A guiding force. He felt himself slipping into sleep and wondered if this was all he was meant to do.

He shivered; it was cold. The ghost was gone, though there was a smell in the air of whisky, and aftershave, and soap. It was night outside, and that darkness with the flapping of the fan brought the bats to mind again. He curled up and wept with grief for those bats, lost generations, and for his father, who had killed them, and his grandfather, and for himself, because he had been a child.

He slept.

He dreamed his mother was burning the dinner and the smell woke him. There was smoke in the room, it was full of smoke and he could hear sirens and screams and he was hot, now. Flames licked under the door. He wrapped the sheet around his waist and ran to the window. It was bolted shut, double glazed. He found his shoe and hammered the window, coughed, coughed, his eyes streamed and his lungs burnt, he choked and coughed and collapsed, he could not draw breath and he could feel his eyes clouding, feel the heat leaving his body, then all was black.

He awoke feeling nothing. He wore his own clothing again and he felt cool, as if a breeze washed over him. He curled up, enjoying the comfort of the bed.

He curled up.

He had not been able to do that for some time. He felt flexible. He stretched out his arms, lifting them high.

"How do you feel?" Jason said. Theo had forgotten his existence, had not heard him enter the room, or, even, knew if he'd left.

"I don't know," said Theo. There was no guilt, he did know that. And the grief was gone, the sorrow for the death of the bats. There was room for something else.

It seemed the ache in his stomach was gone, and his veins didn't hurt.

"Give it a few days."

"I thought I died. There was a fire . . . did someone put it out? Is everyone all right? What about Cameron, is she okay?"

"There was a fire," Jason said. "We discovered that if we trick the body into believing it has died, it will recover from any fatal disease. We've had particular success with cancer. So we placed you behind a death's door, and we physically, in actuality, re-created the death. You *did* die. You took some of the suffering of those who have passed before you, especially him."

"I feel as if the world must have changed," Theo said. "I feel so different, the world must have changed."

"You are a poetic man. But yes. This will suck the spiritual energy from all surrounds. You'll notice everyone around will be feeling lethargic for a day or two. We like to complete the process on Sunday evenings best. People pass off their reaction as Monday-itis."

Jason handed Theo a wallet with $500. "To get you started. Good luck. I've put my card in there. You're welcome to come back if and when you need to. We don't encourage debauchery of the body, but… well, this gives you the freedom to explore without the concerns others have. You will need to consider the financial element. For each visit we require at least double the last. Obviously, all you possess, but it needs to far exceed the amount you paid this time."

He led Theo to the back door.

"Could I say goodbye? I feel as if I know them all so well. And thank the waiters. They're so kind. And to Cameron."

"Best not," Jason said. "Not all of them will pass through the door. It's best for them not to know for sure until…"

The air outside smelt good; someone was cooking onions. He suddenly felt hungry. "A hamburger," he said to himself. "No, a steak."

He felt better the next day, and the next, then he saw his doctor.

"I'd call it a miracle if I believed in them," said the doctor. "But I don't. Good luck. Make the most of your second chance."

Theo did. He met and married a recovering drug addict who never needed another drink or another drug. He didn't invite any of his family to the wedding; as far as they were concerned he had disappeared.

He didn't miss them.

There were times, though, when a spinning fan made a light flicker, or when his ears picked up conversations he shouldn't hear, that he thought of the bat cave and its cold comfort and he did miss that, with an ache he could not ease.

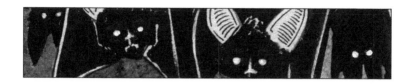

DEATH'S DOOR CAFÉ: A COMMENTARY

IN THE TRADITION OF THE "FOUNTAIN OF YOUTH" story trope of life extension, in "Death's Door Café," Warren takes the common expression for waning health—"knocking on death's door"—literally, offering up an imaginary secret restaurant that serves its clientele a second chance at life by choosing to step behind a number of creative doorways . . . for a price.

As we learn more about Theo's desperate situation, we also learn about his traumatic relationship to death, via a childhood experience involving the massacre of "millions" of bats occupying a cave on his family property. This haunts him even as he passes through the doorway to seek a new chance at a cancer-free life, like many he has seen exit the restaurant before him, in envy. The story is a powerful examination of humanity, dramatizing the eager human yearning for life, and the way in which moral choices imbue life with meaning and hope. The process by which life is extended here ingeniously relies upon ghostly possession of victims of unjust death to allow for a more humane kind of escape from a natural death process.

But what we might miss upon first read of this story are the subtle references to warfare and particularly the Holocaust, as the café's public face is named after the German city of "Dusseldorf" while its doorway includes a memorial to a "Soldier" of unknown nationality. It is odd that the main chamber door for the process one must enter is called "The Gladiator," until one considers the Roman forums, a nod to ancient combat and the legacy of empire. Theo's guilt over the extermination of an excessive number of bats in his youth dimly echoes the cold Nazi murder of millions of Jews during World War II. This might explain why Theo's guilt stays with him in the tale's final lines. Some sins cannot be entirely purged or forgotten. Death is stronger than its doorway.

—Michael Arnzen, PhD

The Wrong Seat

AFTER HER DEATH, MOIRA BRADDON CAUGHT THE
6:00 p.m. Sunday bus, a three hour trip, every week without fail.
She sought sense amongst the passengers who travelled with her;
looked for signs they had been affected by her death. She
wondered which of the women it could have been, which of the
women who travelled every week could have been in an aisle seat
and fallen victim instead of Moira. She was lost and confused; she
hated these people because she meant nothing to them and she
loved them because they were everything to her.

She loved the man who had been sitting in her seat when she
had climbed on the bus at five to 6:00. It was her seat; the ticket
said so. As an experienced traveler, she knew that booking in early
and boarding late meant a good window seat and less crowding.
Yet Moira, weak after a soul-destroying weekend, smiled at the
man who had the window seat. She sat in the aisle seat and the
man settled comfortably.

She would have loved someone to talk to, perhaps to make
laugh, about her disastrous weekend. But she couldn't tell her
travelling companion. She couldn't tell anyone. There was no one
who would listen to her, not avidly. Not with interest, because her
single status was of concern to no one but herself. Twenty-eight
years of age and even a dirty weekend was beyond her, her trip
away a failed attempt at romance. An embarrassing failure; she
had overestimated his interest. She had taken kindness and pity
for lust, and built up the relationship in her mind until a late trip

on Friday night and an appearance on the door step seemed a logical, inevitable step.

She had stayed at the hotel the full weekend out of pride. At his shocked (appalled, really, even terrified) face, his inability to pretend to be happy, she lied. "I've come to see a friend, just thought I'd pop in to say hello."

"Hello," he said. "Nice to see you." He did not lid his eyes in lust, although her silk shirt clung about her breasts and was tied to reveal her smooth, brown belly.

She wore the silk shirt all weekend; she only left her room to buy snacks from the foyer, and she watched videos and snacked until it was time to check out at ten in the morning. Then she wandered town all day, pretending to have someone to meet, waving and smiling at people who weren't there, so that others would think she wasn't alone. It was beyond understanding, her lack of popularity. She was pretty enough, and she tried so hard not to let people down. No matter what they wanted, she smiled and said yes, yet she remained lonely.

She climbed on the bus at five to 6:00.

Uninterested in the movie playing, an old adventure story, shown on a TV so badly magnetized the color was three diagonal bands of green, gray, and red, but she watched it all the same.

The man next to her stared out the window. Once, Moira laughed at a joke in the movie. She leaned to him, so they could laugh together, but his face pulled into a wince of irritation.

She watched the movie and waited for the trip to end.

It was someone on their way to the toilet who killed her. Leaned over and slit her throat. He leaned over, and she smiled at him, thinking he was about to kiss her and wondering why, but still happy to be kissed so spontaneously.

At first she didn't realize what he had done. She felt a coldness across her throat, thought it was his touch and thrilled to its alien nature.

She opened her eyes but he was gone.

She gurgled in surprise. They were very close to home. She was in pain, but she didn't understand why. She touched the man at her side, wanting him to look at her, tell her what was wrong, but he shifted his arm away.

He grunted irritably at the noise she was making, the snuffling and the dripping.

She felt for her handbag, absurdly wanting to show the driver her ticket before she asked for help.

The bag was gone, and she felt cheated. That was all this was about? A small amount of money and some over-used credit cards? She thought about the letter she had written to a friend, detailing graphically and falsely her sexual activities of the weekend. Her killer would read that and think it true, perhaps, then regret killing such a woman. Or he would laugh at it, remember her eager, reaching face and laugh.

The man who killed her got out at the first city stop.

She stood up just as the driver was going around a corner, lost her balance and pressed her hand onto someone's shoulder. They hissed.

She discovered standing and walking were not possible anyway; she was weak.

Her breasts were slick with blood. She felt constrained, and tugged weakly at the buttons of the shirt till they slipped out of their holes.

She spread her shirt open. The man next to her glanced at her, but saw perhaps a dark singlet. The unhealthy glow of the flickering street lights did not aid vision. And if she could not understand her state, how could he?

She wondered if they would call her Moira Braddon, or if her name would become The Passenger in 6B—or 6A, as her ticket said.

When the lights came on as the bus rolled into the depot, the man who had taken her seat looked at her and shouted, "You stupid bitch," though how it was her fault he didn't say.

Nobody wanted to stay around with a dead body on board. They were off the bus and waiting for their luggage before Moira could sneeze. They collected bags, and left. Names were a matter of record, addresses the manager took, apologizing for the inconvenience. People were annoyed, then. They felt guilty at first, then when they were told how inconvenient it was they were annoyed. They went off into the night, home to where no bodies lay.

The man who had not known she was dying was allowed to go as well.

Moira caught the 6:00 p.m. bus the following Sunday because she was tired of hanging around the depot. She wandered up and down the aisle; she didn't know what to do. She sat on the laps of people who had window seats and stared out. She kicked the back of the chair in front but the person did not wake up.

She would have liked to see her funeral but she couldn't seem to leave the depot or the bus. It would have been a dismally attended affair; she couldn't pretend otherwise. Her mother would have cried and the others would have waited till it was over and left. She always wanted to be cremated but hoped her mother hadn't listened. It didn't seem as final, now, being popped into the ground.

She caught the Sunday bus again.

Each time, there were familiar faces; passengers from the trip where she died. She never saw the man who killed her; he was somewhere else now. She wouldn't see him again. She wouldn't close her eyes for a kiss. She forgot him; and he had touched her in a way no one else had.

Finally, the man who had sat next to her was on board. He had a window seat again.

She leaned over the woman in the aisle seat—a middle-aged

woman reading a book with deep interest. She stared at the man who had let her die; who hadn't notice her vanishing.

He stared out the window. Moira twisted herself around until she could see directly into his eyes. She looked there for some image, a picture of herself snapped there, or some reason for his inactivity. His nose wrinkled. He glanced at the middle-aged woman as if imagining the smell came from her. But her nose wrinkled too.

"Must be the toilet," she said, although the occupied light had not shown so far on the journey.

Moira was distressed to learn that she smelt. She had always been very clean, her clothes and her body. She didn't catch any buses for a while but found she was very lonely at the depot. She would just begin to enjoy the warmth of a person and they would catch their bus. At least when she journeyed with them she could have them for longer.

After a while, she didn't care about her stink. She would sit next to people who had an empty seat, sit there and talk to them as if they were real. Some would breathe into a palm to see if it was their breath.

Moira grinned into their faces, waiting for them to notice her.

She left her shoes behind and wore her stockinged feet. She climbed onto the backs of seats and waved her feet under their noses.

She grew to need those looks of disgust, because they meant she existed.

Walking naked up and down the aisle, she bent and breathed into the faces of the sleepers, breathing into their dreams, giving them nightmares of cesspits and poison.

She liked to lie down in the aisle as they got off. The people walked over her and she raised her arms to let them smell her sweat. They climbed off quickly when she lay there, like they had when she had died on the journey, when she was carried off on the last night of her life.

It was good when the videos were running, because she could watch the screen, and the people's eyes were open and staring. She tried to see herself reflected, but they always blinked too soon.

Whenever the man who had ignored her death was on the bus she spent the whole trip with him. He always had the window seat, and it took her a while to realize that he was staring at his reflection, not the dark world flashing by.

She sat between his toes, or stood leaning over him. She breathed deeply of him and he began to get used to her smell.

He usually sat alone because people would ask to move. They thought the smell was him.

She breathed into his ear. She said, "How was it my fault? Why blame me? Didn't you see him? Why did you let me bleed and die? I bled and died without you turning your head. Didn't you smell my blood? Where are you going? Where are you going? Where do you go?" She followed him to the door of the bus and waved him goodbye like a lover. He always took a few steps away from her, stopped, took deep lungsful of air. He sucked air that didn't smell of her, and she wandered up and down the aisles of the buses, her breath redolent of rotten teeth, the air in her wake like diarrhea, her underarms like years of grime.

The last time she clung onto his back like the old man in the sea, wrapped her legs around his waist, her arms around his neck, hoping that she could go with him that way.

He pushed other people aside to get off the bus, seeking the air outside. He pushed hard, rudely and blindly, and as he ran down the steps the other passengers collectively pushed back. He was thrown from the bus and landed with his head against a pole; he did not move.

Moira looked at him and thought, "Enough."

Then she left, before he could rise and give chase.

THE WRONG SEAT: A COMMENTARY

"THE WRONG SEAT" IS A POTENT WORK OF FLASH fiction, revealing Kaaron Warren's power to use the allegory of fantasy to explore women's issues. A deceptively simple tale about a ghost on a bus, the story packs several complex notions into a very brief tale. Perhaps most importantly, "The Wrong Seat" explores female identity, by telling the tale of an isolated woman "trapped" in her role as a passive passenger in the afterlife and the steps she takes to acquire a kind of freedom.

It is important that this story is told from the dead woman's perspective. Most tales about a ghost who haunts a particular place are not so much about the haunted space but about *justice*—the revenant spirit cannot be freed from its shackles to a particular place until a crime against it has been avenged or the culprit's secret brought to light. Typically, the ghost, or its motives, is a kind of secret that the protagonists must discover if they hope to survive.

In this story, the protagonist is the ghost itself, who must discover how to survive on her own. Moira has been randomly victimized and ignored by the other people on the bus: the whole bus—mostly composed of rude and selfish men—is complicit in the crime against her.

Radically displaced from her role as a passive passenger in her life, the sort willing to give her bus seat over to a bully, she progressively learns to not only endure her boredom in the purgatory of her situation, but to more actively appreciate her newfound powers as a ghost. In other words, as the story progresses, she reclaims her identity. It doesn't matter if she escapes her place in the bus or not in the story's ending; what matters is that she has escaped her own passivity, when she has had "enough." The woman who is trapped on the bus is a stand-in for all women who might be trapped in their assumptions about what is proper, attractive, and required of being a good woman, when it means being a passive victim.

—Michael Arnzen, PhD

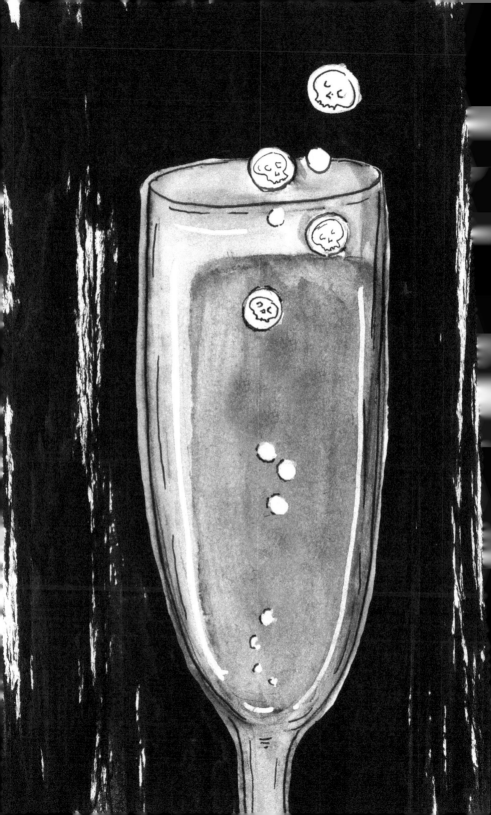

SINS OF THE ANCESTORS

CLIENTS LIKE TO DIE IN DIFFERENT WAYS.
Yolanda was no longer surprised by the methods they chose. She
pulled on thick gloves and stood, naked, in front of the mirror.

"I look ridiculous," she muttered. She glared at herself, trying
to look like a killer.

He was waiting upstairs, sitting on the lounge, watching TV. A
bowl of peanuts on his lap, large glass of white wine (not red. There'd
be enough stains for his cleaners to deal with if she did her job right).

She pulled on a pair of boots for height, flexed her fingers,
slipped on a robe and walked upstairs on the tips of her toes, not
wanting to alert him. Some of them preferred a warning, others
wanted sudden, choking fear.

His head was slumped forward and she could hear his deep,
congested breathing.

Sleeping.

She nodded, steeling herself, then walked up to him and
dropped her robe. He didn't stir.

She stepped sideways, poured herself a brandy, tossed it back,
all while eyeing him off, placing him.

He wasn't a government man. Most of them were too scared
of exposure to use a service like hers.

A company man, then. Sugar? She leant close to him and sniffed.

Tobacco. She recognized him now, from the social pages. His
skin was sallow. You couldn't tell that from the photos. His hair
was lank, sitting on his shoulders like old corn silk.

He'd paid good money to risk his life being with her, and he looked almost dead anyway.

She readied her fingers around his throat.

She straddled him. He stirred. She bit his lip, tightening her fingers around his neck. He shifted, but she had his arms pinned to his sides with her thighs.

"You should be careful who you bring home," she said, because that was part of his fantasy; he was a risk-taker, picking up a woman, not caring about her Ancestor ID, taking her home.

She squeezed tighter and he began to fight for real, now.

"You should have checked my ID. My ancestor was a murderer. Tried, convicted, dead by firing squad. What do you think that makes me?"

Her client's eyelids fluttered and she took that as a sign to stop. She loosened her grip on his throat, stepped off him and poured another brandy. It was the expensive kind; only high-level careers could afford it.

He lit a cigarette and turned the TV up.

"Money?" she said. He pointed at a sideboard, a huge pre-ID piece he must have inherited.

She and her brother Theo had only inherited bad blood.

The money, old, dirty notes which looked like they'd been used to clean a toilet. "Take it, you piece of shit."

She looked at him, sitting in his stained underwear, stinking of smoke and sweat, his fat white flesh unhealthy.

Yet I'm shit, she thought.

"You can fuck off now," he said, throwing the full ashtray at her. It hit her on the chin, bringing tears to her eyes.

She pulled on her robe. She'd shower downstairs, once he'd sunk into the TV.

He watched her. "You could have killed me. You don't look big enough to have strong fingers like that."

She mimed twisting. "I kill a lot of chickens."

It was what he paid for; the moment of fear when it could all end for him.

Because men like him, they really did believe that murderer descendants are easily capable of murder themselves.

"Next time you eat a chicken, think of me," she said.

She called Theo and waited for him under the small shelter the doorway provided. There were places in the world where you could be warm outside. She'd read about them. Places where they didn't judge you on who your ancestors were and what they did.

She checked her face in the mirror. The mark from the ashtray was clearly visible.

"How the hell did you get that? Don't worry. Don't answer. You need to stop what you're doing. It's bad for the body and for your soul." Theo drove angrily. She knew he was angry because he was helpless.

"Next client is Oster Wu," she said.

He tutted. "You should rest between, at least."

"Who has time to rest? You can wait downstairs. He doesn't mind. Use the shower, make a coffee."

Theo wrinkled his face. "But then I'll hear you. I don't like to hear you."

"You can block your ears. You need a shower and coffee will do you good, too."

The curtain fluttered as they arrived. Oster Wu liked to be ready; Yolanda took some heavy-duty painkillers, preparing herself for what would come.

Oster Wu picked up her shirt and cleaned himself up with it, then handed it to her.

"You should clean yourself, come to the Arena today."

"I can't afford to go to the Arena!"

He opened his wallet. "Here. A pass. For you and your killer brother, too." He smiled. He'd asked Yolanda to bring Theo along to their sessions; he liked the idea of more than one assassin.

She'd never agree. Shove the money.

"You don't need to protect me," Theo had said, furious when he realized what she shielded him from, while putting herself in it.

"Looking out for you is the only worthwhile thing I'm ever likely to do. So let me do it."

Oster waved money in her face.

"I really don't like these shows."

He moved quickly, grabbing her throat.

"I'll pay you. I want you to be there. To see it. There's two going down today. Both mine. I want you to see it." He was proud of his work at the Department of Unsolved Crime.

"All right, all right, I'll go."

"And you'll pay attention."

Yolanda scrubbed his blood off her arms, her face, her hair. He liked to bleed on her bare skin.

"So he's paying us? That's why we're going?" Theo asked.

"You know I'll do anything for money."

"I don't know why going to these shows bothers you so much, anyway."

"It's the implications," she said, as Theo drove. He liked to drive with just a finger on the wheel; only the fact that the car practically drove itself saved them three or four times.

She curled herself up in the front seat.

"What implications? What do you care if a killer dies?"

"Descendant of a killer. Of an alleged killer. This is an innocent person."

"With guilty blood. You can't deny that. They have the evidence."

"We have that blood ourselves, Theo."

"Yes, but our ancestor paid the price. We will not have to pay for it. God, would you look at that sky? Perfect execution weather," Theo said.

"It's always like this." Gray and cold, the sun a pale star. "What would it be like to live in a warm place, do you reckon?"

"Wouldn't be good execution weather."

They were six blocks from the execution hall when traffic blocked them. Theo looked for a parking spot.

"Drop me off at the door. I don't want to walk all that way."

"It's okay for me to walk so far, is it? I'll miss the show if I have to drive through that to drop you off. You'll walk with me."

"I'll get out here, then," she said. She didn't like to tell him, but this was a fine time to find new clients. Not so many men came to the executions. Of the ones who did, there was always one or two who would like to use her services.

Busloads of spectators arrived.

She watched Theo drive off, then turned and walked toward the arena. The footpath was slick and slimy with a reddish sheen to it as it often was after the rain.

Crowds of women walked past, rushing into the arena, not wanting to miss a moment.

What was it that made women so interested in the death of another? she thought.

Inside the arena, it was hot. Yolanda's hair went limp and her clothes were wet in a moment.

"Where's the air conditioning?" someone yelled.

"Shut down. Can't cope with the heat," and that was all very funny, but who could breath in there?

The crowd roared, conversations piling one on the other until the din sounded like a chicken yard before the killing began.

The air smelt of pine needles. The smell of sweat, too, hundreds of bodies soaked through. Vomit, from the heat and the drink.

Yolanda tucked her arms into her body, made herself small. The jostle and press of the place was oppressive. She wished she was outdoors.

The lights dimmed and people quieted, lone voices shushed. A spotlight on centre stage showed a bright red armchair with large purple cushions.

The crowd hushed as the announcer spoke. "Sonny May, you are charged with your ancestor's unpunished crime of the murder of thirteen women over a nine year period. You have chosen to die by dream sleep. What is your selected dream death?"

Sonny May's voice started creakily and he had to clear his throat. "I want to dream of dying while having sex with a beautiful woman."

The audience laughed, enjoying this.

In the next section she saw Oster Wu, his face bright, his clothing loose. She knew he'd had a lot to do with bringing Sonny May to justice. Oster liked her to break into his home, carrying a gun. He liked to disarm her, take her down.

She turned her head, not wanting to speak to him. She'd asked him for a favor; access to files she shouldn't see. She was waiting for his answer, but this was not the place to remind him.

Theo found her, gave her a wink.

The executioner entered the dream death and gestured Sonny May to sit in the armchair.

"This'll be good," Theo whispered to her. He was agitated. Excited. Most of the men were; she could tell by the way they fidgeted.

Sonny May sat down and was strapped into the chair. His hat was removed. He was bald, beneath.

The executioner applied lubricant to his temples then attached the transmitter, adjusting it so it didn't slip and choke him.

"Do you have any last words?"

Sonny May looked at the audience. "Just that this is my ancestor's crime, not mine, and that I have three children who are also innocent."

"Exodus, Chapter 20, Verse 5. 'For I the Lord thy God am a jealous God, visiting the iniquity of the fathers upon the children unto the third and fourth generation of them that hate me.'"

Sonny May had lived an easy life. No label on him, because the crime had remained unsolved until recently. He could have done anything, gone anywhere.

And yet he'd wasted that freedom, staying in his own little place and doing nothing but have children.

At that moment, Yolanda hated him with jealousy-filled fury.

"Are there any registered descendants of the long-dead victims of this family?" the announcer called. One man stood up.

"I am."

"Do you wish to close-witness the death?"

"I do not."

The crowd hissed. What was he, an objector? He should stay home, then.

The executioner set the dreamer going. Sonny pulled back from the temporal impact, then relaxed into it.

His face slackened. His lips puckered. He wriggled in the chair.

The medic nodded. The executioner started the drip which would stop the blood in its tracks.

Some in the audience hissed more.

"Why can't they let him die his own way?" Yolanda said.

"They think this dream death is too good for killers."

"If the Victims' Lobby Party say it's okay, they should accept that."

Sonny May stiffened. Close up shots of him showed that he appeared to be approaching orgasm. Then he slumped.

An extreme close up of his face showed a tear in his eye, and an expression on his face Yolanda recognized.

It was the look people give when a terrible truth dawns on them.

On the wall, above the commentary box, sat a counter, indicating the number of seconds it took for him to die.

Assistants dressed in black wheeled Sonny off stage, through the audience and out of the arena. Some leaned in for a better look; others pulled back.

Yolanda tucked her head under her arm.

She felt a tap on her shoulder. A big man stood there, two heads taller than she was. His shirt barely covered his stomach, which stuck, white and hairy, over the top of his pants.

He thrust a large wad of notes in her hand.

"Toilets. Now."

She shook her head. He leaned in.

"Oster Wu sent me. I'm a file clerk."

She was quick enough to know what this meant.

He had access to the files she wanted to see.

She nodded. "I'll be back soon," she whispered in Theo's ear.

The man handed her a knife. Security was always lax in the arena.

"He doesn't know you're coming. I want to give that bastard Oster Wu a scare, a real scare. You do this, I can help you out."

Yolanda hated unknowns. They were dangerous, because people thinking on their feet always were.

She needed the file clerk's help, though.

She slipped quickly through the crowd, knowing her only chance was surprise. Crouching down low, the knife ready. In the crowd she nicked a leg, saw the blood drip appear, moved on.

Oster watched the stage. He was short, had to stand on his toes to see.

She stepped up behind him, pulled his hair back and held the knife to his throat.

"Money, fucker," she whispered.

"Die, bitch." He twisted out of her grip easily and punched her, full-fisted, on the face.

The pain blacked her out for a split second but she had the sense to turn and run.

The file clerk grabbed her around the throat.

"Kill her, killer, kill her." Oster Wu hissed. She felt wet all over. One of them pissed on her, one of them spat, no one noticed and no one cared.

The file clerk twisted her neck and she sucked air, suffocating.

"Let her go. Stop now," Oster Wu said. She fell, panting for air, to the floor amongst the vomit, piss, spilled drinks.

"Can't kill my best girl," Wu said.

The interval. A bar surrounded the arena with a hundred bartenders pouring good, solid, old fashioned drinks like gin tonic, vodka orange, brandy dry. Service was quick and efficient; you could easily manage three drinks in the interval if you drank quickly.

The lights flickered. "Testing the equipment," someone called. People laughed; Yolanda couldn't see how that was funny.

"Seats, please. Seats please. The execution of Mele Dova will begin in twelve minutes."

A rush for the bar; most people liked to sit down with a drink in either hand.

They heard the screaming first.

"This'll be interesting," Theo whispered. "When they fight it. The ones who just take it aren't much fun."

Forget about dignity in death then, Yolanda thought.

The announcer said, "You should all have a dream death in mind. The technology is available to citizens, not just convicted descendants. You can die in bed, on a mountain top, you can die with a mouthful of your favorite food. You can die after saying goodbye, making amends."

"None of us have that kind of money," Theo said.

Mele Dova screamed as they wheeled her down the aisle, strapped in a wheelchair. A brace held her head still, but they hadn't gagged her.

"What's wrong with her?" Yolanda asked Oster Wu, who had loosened his belt and had his hands down there.

"I heard she was useless below the waist."

But Yolanda could see her legs straining against the binding.

"With this death, we apologize for the sin of murder. We hope this apology will help to lift the curse on this country. Mele Dova, you are charged with the murders of eighteen patients, victims of your nurse-ancestor. You failed to select a method of execution, so it has been decided you should die in the manner of your ancestors. Are there any registered descendants of the long dead victims of this family?"

Two women called out, "We are."

"And do you wish to close-witness this execution?"

"Yes."

They ran to the stage, making people laugh at their eagerness. They stood in front of Mele Dova, staring into her eyes. She began to cry. "I'm sorry, I'm sorry, I'm sorry."

They always cried when confronted with the victim's descendants.

They wheeled the electric chair down the aisle.

The audience screamed, a contagion of noise which set them all off.

"I don't want to watch this," Yolanda said. She had seen many terrible things in her life; had done some, caused some. But this . . .

She hid her head under Theo's arm. Let him tease her about it later.

The minutes passed. The counter said 18:06 but it felt like a lot more than eighteen minutes, watching the woman die.

The victim descendants moaned and cried. Close up, it was even worse. Mele Dova had no dignity in death. She burned, fried, stiffened, stank, all with the audience watching, breathless. She ground her teeth so hard she dribbled spots of enamel onto her chin.

It was so cold outside Yolanda felt the wax in her ears crackle. She wanted to curl up somewhere and cry, away from the world.

She found the car and waited for Theo. Around her, people were enlivened, walking quickly, a bounce in their step.

"The air! The air is good! Cleaner!" they shrieked to each other.

"What dream death would you choose? I know some women would like to die in childbirth," Theo said, opening the car.

"Who wants kids? They'd only be labeled like we are."

"We have a right to children."

"Having a right doesn't mean you have to exercise it," Yolanda said. "I'd choose to die in a plane crash, on my way to some wonderful place. When it's still perfect, still about the possibilities."

"I'd die in the water. Warm water, the sun beating down, salty water you can feel on your skin. That's how I'd die."

"You did well at the execution," Oster Wu said. It was warm in his house. Wonderful to be warm inside. In the car, the wind chill factor dropped, but it was so very cold.

"Someone has to pay, isn't that right?"

He smiled. It was the police motto. Half the city's population were cops.

He unzipped his pants, and she hid her revulsion.

"When are we going to travel for the weekend? Or the week? Think of the danger you could be in, travelling with me like that," she said.

There were certain privileges awarded to All Clears. Access to restaurants high in the mountains, where she'd heard the food was made for the Gods.

Unrestricted Travel.

Air Travel.

There were benefits.

"You can't travel, Yolanda."

"You could help me to. I'll kill you in Venice. I'll kill you on the beach, in an old crypt, I'll murder you on a hilltop and slit your throat on an ocean cruise."

A red spot of color appeared on his cheeks. "My mate was pretty impressed with you."

"So he'll help me?"

"He'll help *me*. But he was impressed. He'll arrange for you to look at the records. That's all. Just to see if there's a flaw somewhere. Some people have had their ancestors' convictions overturned. If you find a flaw, they'll do the molec test. They wouldn't have done it at the time."

She knew that the molec test read molecular vibrations. Each person has one, and leaves a trace very easily. Each one is unique and there is a unique crossover between killer and victim. It is unmistakable. Inarguable.

"I don't know why you're bothering. You're lucky. Your ancestor was punished for the crime. You won't be executed for it."

She said, "I'm uneducated, unskilled, and the only men who'll sleep with me are the sick fucks who think I might just kill them.

Some of them are disappointed to be still alive when it's all over, I think."

He'd already lost interest, though, and he flipped open a newspaper to look for mentions of himself.

It gave her some space. Thirty minutes alone, to sit in the warm and quiet, to think.

Weeks later, she went to the file clerk's house. She had to do him first, but he liked it simple, straight sex, no violence. One of the easy ones.

"I wanted to be a cop but they wouldn't take me, fat arse that I am. They're the fucken' heroes of this world. I tell you. Look at the crime rates. Lowest since record-taking began. I'll show you how to log on. You'll look at your records, and your records alone. If you look at anybody else's records I'll be able to track your downloads and you'll be prosecuted, no doubt of that."

"But . . ." she stroked his hand. "What about you? I mean, this isn't a threat, but if I go down, they'll trace it to you."

He shook his head. "I'm logging you in through nine different routes."

Strange how the details of history are lost. The names of minor players, whose actions have great affect on the way events play out. The guards who let in the assassin who killed a king; their names are forgotten, though surely they affected the future with their laziness.

Decisions are blurred, too; small level politics which affect many major decision are not noted or registered. The lunch which won a vote, the accident which lost one.

Yolanda understood this as she read her ancestor's files. She could see poor research, interviews unfinished, and a local area study questionnaire mostly marked "To Be Completed".

Yet her ancestor Paul Friedham had been convicted. Checking the dates against recorded events she saw that, during his investigation, there was a sniper at large, targeting police officers.

Not only would this have distracted the police from other investigations, but there was mention of her ancestor as a possible associate of one of five suspects. Both of them homosexual and, in those times, therefore instantly untrustworthy.

That was enough, it seemed, to convict and put him to death.

But his elsewhere excuse was perfect. Someone had written 'unchecked' across the photo. All the photos were archived; Yolanda found the original event, a concert of musical opera, and there was the photo, with her ancestor in the audience.

Much was made in the press of how an uncle had taken Paul in as a teenager, against all warnings. "He's flighty, untrustworthy," people said. But the uncle took him in. The uncle, father to fourteen, a legendarily fertile man, was a great proponent of children in marriage and caring for blood.

Yolanda wrote her letter carefully, ensuring any hint of desperation was removed. She stated her case, presented the facts, enclosed copies of the evidence. Theo called her a fool to stir things up. "You're happy enough, aren't you? You should be grateful for what we have." He had a new lover, and all was right in his world.

Then she waited. She carried on with her life. Days driving around, nights with customers. It was often Oster, forever a freebie after all he'd done for her.

She felt great self-hatred after each session. She wished she had the power, the guts, to really kill them, but she never would.

She'd go to Theo in the car and he'd hold her while she cried. He'd count the money and talk about what they'd spend it on, and he'd feed her little crumbs of chocolate he stole from a café.

Every morning she covered her bruises, dressed, and checked her post office box.

No letter came. She'd been told, don't call, don't email, don't show up in person. Just wait. You'll know when you'll know, and then you'll know.

Others had received their assessments (always no; almost always no) in nine weeks.

It was fifteen weeks later when she was awoken in the car by two Ancestral Police, in red uniforms.

"Step out of the car, please. Yolanda Friedham?" one said. His voice was soft and gentle; it made Yolanda smile. She nodded, climbing out of the car.

"Yolanda Friedham, your application for reassessment of ancestral crime has been received," the other said.

She smiled. Still smiling.

"The files have been assessed and molecular vibrations taken. I will read the result of the reinvestigation to you. Your ancestor, Paul Friedham, has been found not guilty."

Before she could speak, though, before she could cheer and jump, kiss the Ancestral Police (*but why were they there?* This ran through her head, right underneath the happiness, the thoughts of freedom), the AP said, "However, investigation of this offence and the reassessment has brought to light further evidence, leading to the identification of the actual perpetrator of the homicide."

Yolanda realized the other AP had stepped very close to her.

"And?" she said. Her voice felt hard in her throat.

"The identified perpetrator is Thomas Friedham, uncle of Paul Friedham, founder of Freedom Food, the charity. There is latter-day evidence of corruption at high levels in local government, the police department, and the courts."

The AP smiled, as if unsurprised by this example of human nature. He read, "As this renders the crime unpunished, under ancestral law Thomas Friedham's most direct descendant will be charged and executed."

The AP said, "We inherit the material wealth of our ancestors. We must pay for their sins, as well."

Yolanda had thought herself a strong woman. Unlucky and strong.

Now she realized she had been neither.

Yolanda sipped champagne, gazing out at the sea below. The flight attendant, realizing this was her first flight, was very kind, explaining things to her, giving her drinks and food, making sure she didn't feel nervous.

Beside her, Theo flicked through a magazine, smiling at her every now and again.

"Happy?"

"Of course."

The plane dropped slightly, and the passengers gasped, grabbing each other.

The pain began in her toes, an ache she attributed to cabin pressure. Then her shins, her thighs, her hips, and once it hit her spine, the agony was too much to bear. The agony took her out, took her off the plane and into the arena where she knew, she really knew and had to admit that her plane would never land.

SINS OF THE ANCESTORS: A COMMENTARY

WE ALL ARE FATED BY OUR BODIES, BY THE TRAITS passed down to us by our DNA, and we are all fated to die. This physical die-casting is one of the reasons why social hierarchies, especially those that put people in their place due solely to the "crime" of gender differences, are an unfair and arbitrary cruelty. "Sins of the Ancestors" is a depressing science fiction story about this topic on its surface, telling a tale of a prostitute trying to escape her social conditions by playing to the death fantasies of the culture she was born into, a culture she is destined to be punished by due to her physical heritage. But its ending still manages to offer a glimmer of hope in the psychological escape from social cruelty that her fantasy allows.

It is important that her occupation as a kind of role-playing prostitute—serving the perverse near-death fantasies of men who not only dehumanize her but also essentially abuse her even if she is hired to abuse them—is one that finds power in fantasy itself. In the end, it is *her* own fantasy—the "dream death"—where she finally achieves a kind of happiness, even if fleeting, that she earns through subverting the patriarchal system that would—and inevitably does—punish her for no crime of her own. On another, more metafictional, level, we shouldn't ignore the fact that this story is *itself* a fantasy, written by a woman, and that her lesson related to dream deaths and escape is also one about fantasy *literature* as well, because of it.

—Michael Arnzen, PhD

CRISIS APPARITION

THE BELIEVERS TROOPED THROUGH SHAWN'S kitchen, each of them holding a tray ready for the food he'd cooked. He was embarrassed to face them; the meal wasn't good. Moses insisted it be bland, with no stimulating flavors like onion or garlic. Ginger was the only spice allowed, because it provided healing at a physical and soulful level, so Shawn used it, wild and cultivated, as much as he could.

They all took their plates and carried them through to the lounge room, where they sat at the table, or in arm chairs, or on the floor or the balcony. Shawn made a lot of food and twice as much rice as he thought was required, learning from past experience there were always those who took more than they needed and didn't care if there wasn't any left at the end for the slower ones. So was the case this time; the last woman to hold out her tray smiled ruefully as he piled it high with rice.

"Not much else left, I'm afraid," he said as he ladled the last of the sauce onto her plate.

"That's okay. I'm not really hungry," she said. She reminded him a bit of his late wife around the eyes, and she wore her hair in a high ponytail as his wife had done.

Earlier, Shawn had doled out and put aside two plates of food for the elderly couple who lived downstairs, above his own small apartment. They'd been in the apartment block forever. Once they owned the whole place, he'd heard, but they'd sold it off room by room, floor by floor.

He carried the plates to their apartment. They often left their front door open, forgetting that they shared the space with strangers. They had all their groceries delivered (sometimes they paid Shawn to do it) and their only sunlight came in through a single dirty window.

Shawn wondered what the point was, living their lives out like that. God knows what they thought went on in the basement, or on the top floor where Moses lived and preached, and where Shawn cooked for the believers.

He placed the plates on their kitchen table. He liked to feed them and Moses had never asked him not to. If the old lady caught him she'd insist on giving him something, an ancient piece of cake or a carton of cream long since gone solid. Shawn was certain the food he brought them was the only food they ate.

Moses told him that this time, the old couple were attending the combination smoke ceremony and sweat lodge set up in the basement. Shawn thought he should talk the couple out of it. The basement was too many steps down, was the least of it, and for them to be shut in there for an hour, let alone two or three days, seemed wrong.

It wasn't up to him, though. Not up to him to save anybody.

Shawn stood at the door to the basement handing out bottles of water Moses had infused with ginger and other herbs and the pressings of flowers. "God bless you," Shawn told each one, not meaning a word of it. Moses stood beside him, nodding approvingly; he was easy to convince. Counting his disciples in, bestowing mantras upon them (*spiritual names*, he called them) which made them smile as if blessed. All of the names wood-inspired, like Ash, Chestnut, Hickory, Larch. Moses and Shawn had laid the fire earlier with Oleander and Wild Ginger, considered toxic but Moses said that was part of the test. They laid Black Poplar, which shouldn't burn but would in Moses's fire.

"This will be too hot," Shawn had said. Moses shook his head. He did that; shook his head and Shawn would fall silent.

"Give them a taste of the fires of Hell and they'll choose my Heaven," he said.

As the believers walked into the basement Moses said to each one, "Leave yourself behind," and it was true they all looked the same to Shawn, with their white hooded bath robes.

The heavy door slammed shut. Moses had the only key; he'd be the one to let them out, when he decided it was time, unless someone broke the door down.

That was Thursday. Shawn hadn't seen them since, although he could smell smoke drifting up through the cracks.

With the house effectively empty upstairs, he explored. Some had locked their rooms but he had a master key, something he always liked to get hold of wherever he lived. There was poignancy in the things the believers brought with them and this was where he saw who they were, beyond the disciple-masks they wore.

Toys in the children's bedroom. Sunglasses, earrings, silk scarves. Cameras. All of the things they had decided they couldn't live without. He felt an affection for all of them and thought it would be nice to treat them to a good meal, so he took money, ten bucks, twenty, from each room. None of them would miss it. They'd come out blissed to the eyeballs and starving, and money would be the last thing on their minds. In the posh guy's room (Moses had named him *Ash*), Shawn found a suit hanging up on an improvised hook. The material felt soft between his fingers and he reckoned it was about his size so he tried it on. The guy would never know, not in a million. He didn't trust himself, though. He planned to head to the pub after this and God knows what state he'd be in at the end of that session. So he carefully hung the suit back up and left it reluctantly behind. The guy had a few hundred in his wallet and Shawn relieved him of fifty. The guy's girlfriend was only in her twenties, if that. *Witchhazel*, Moses named her. Shawn hated to see them together, the way she worshipped him because he was old.

He was tempted to borrow one of the cameras, show up at the pub with it just for the laughs, but that was a fast way to get caught.

In theory, Shawn had the whole weekend off because the believers were going without food and water until they had a breakthrough, or until Monday morning, whichever came first. Moses had told him to go away, down the coast or into the mountains, have a change of air. He'd said, "Take three days, or four," but he had nowhere to go except the pub.

He turned on a few lights to stop the local busybodies from worrying about *no one home, what's wrong*. They didn't want the police around breaking down doors. God knows what they'd cop Moses for, but Shawn's fingerprints were definitely on the record.

His local pub did a good schnitzel and he knew half the people there, so that was his venue of choice for Saturday night. It was a late opener, too, not kicking them out until after 3 a.m. Shawn was weeping by then; he'd remember this the next day. "I've tried to have a good life," he told the other drinkers.

"You have, mate," they told him, and that brought on the tears.

"That's not what my flatmates reckon," he said, flatmates being the easiest way to describe Moses and the myriad of believers who came through the doors.

"Yeah, well, with friends like those you don't need enemies," the barman said, and Shawn bought another round of drinks with some of the money he'd stolen. "Fuck that guy, taking advantage of you," the barman said, because Shawn had told them he cooked for free, not earning a cent.

"He's ripping you off," the others agreed as they all drank till he had no money left.

He fumbled his car key into the door lock, dropping the key cluster once. He had a rule that if he dropped the keys three times he didn't drive.

As he pulled into the steep driveway he saw the building was dark apart from the lights he'd left on. No one else liked parking there because you had to angle to get out again, but Shawn's car was like an extension of himself.

He called the place *The Black House* when Moses wasn't listening. It had seen many deaths over the decades. Some would say a curse had been laid but Shawn had enough curses laid on him, so he chose to believe the place was just sick, full of death and disease, filth, dust, things left behind by dozens of people in a space under a bed that has never been cleaned. A brass plate on the front door named it *ÉPAVE*, French for *WRECK*.

He'd been in this house for longer than the one he'd shared with his wife, almost as long as his childhood home. He felt tethered to it, stuck, as if leaving would break something in him as long as Moses wanted him to stay.

Shawn had moved homes a lot, more often than most, always leaving stuff behind. Whatever he carried, or was in his car, that's what he took with him. He got tired of places, began to feel unwelcome in them, imagining the walls clogged with mold, the cracks filled with his own detritus, the halls run thick with ghosts looking for help.

He knew that Moses gave him the job out of gratitude. Out of pity. But Shawn wished he could break away. It suited Moses to be the better man, to have Shawn to compare himself to, to show his believers where any of them could end up without Moses's help.

Shawn thought that Moses got all his luck, and he got nothing.

His room was downstairs, the first room underground. He had his own small door that opened out into the undergrowth. People forgot it was there, if they ever knew.

Shawn let himself in through his secret door and crashed in his bed fully clothed.

He woke up Sunday afternoon at around four and knew he had to get moving. There was shopping to be done, because they'd want breakfast (they'd probably want it at midnight, if they got out by then) and they'd want juices and all the rest of it. They'd drag themselves up the stairs, children being carried, and flop themselves around the large living room, on chairs and the floor. They wouldn't thank him as he gave them food, they wouldn't even see him. No one ever thanked him. Not with the sort of food they were eating, food with no joy in it. All medicinal, from the wild ginger and ginseng he added to every meal, to the seeds and grains he was barely allowed to cook. He headed for the kitchen to remind himself of what he needed.

The third floor was not the usual cacophony of noise. The parents had unbelievably asked him to mind the kids (*Pine, Poplar, Rowan, Spruce, Sycamore*). He'd said no, so they were all down in the sweat lodge. "Five of them under twelve," the mother (*Hawthorn*) told him three or four times, as if she wanted some kind of medal. This family had the best view, out to the ocean. Sunny, too, so less of the mold that grew everywhere else in the house.

He didn't know the rest of his neighbors in the building. They all kept to themselves, kept different hours. The only indication the other apartments were inhabited were the occasional bang and thump, or the sound of the toilet flushing at 3 a.m. They were mostly short-term, disciples coming in for Moses's intensive Heart and Soul Cure weekends and longer retreats.

Above the kitchen and living area, on the covered roof, was the yoga center and meditation hall. Shawn rarely went up there.

A man sat in the corner of the kitchen, hands on his knees, palms up, saying nothing, turning his head away when Shawn said, "G'day." Most of the believers ignored him like that. Pretended he didn't exist.

Shawn opened the fridge to see what he needed to buy. He tried to put a bit of flavor into it all, but there wasn't much he was allowed to use besides ginger. He bought it on the branch and that was what they were burning down in the basement, alongside the oleander root he'd collected for them. He could smell it now, a gingery woody scent. The basement was supposed to be airtight but close enough, he guessed. Ginseng a good one too. If you gave people flavor they felt as if they've eaten more. Moses's shtick was *city living, country health*. He'd say, "Health is where you are. You can't always get away outside the city limits for a weekend of mindfulness and pure water."

Shawn wrote out his shopping list then decided to have a drink before he left. There were always bottles showing up, half this and half that, the believers bringing them along to tip down the sink, make a point, but what a waste, what a waste. Most of the believers who came in were very needy. They'd lost a lot already, or had a lot riding on them to stay on top of things. They had kids and loved ones, people who needed them.

Shawn didn't envy that part of it. He hated to be tethered.

He had a drink before he left, a quick drink before heading to the shops. He couldn't cope otherwise. He mixed whiskey with some of the rainwater he collected in buckets on the rooftop. They liked everything "pure," so rainwater it was, which he'd strain for bugs but not much else. The man in the corner of the kitchen had gone so he didn't have to offer him one.

He had another quick drink to sustain him, then put on the rich man's suit, just to test it out, see if he'd buy one himself, and headed out the front door.

Shawn drove to the shops to buy some milk and something else that he wished he could remember. His toes felt cramped in the shoes he'd put on and, looking down, he saw they were bright pink and far too small for him. At the time it'd been a joke, a funny lark, rushing out the door like that to the sound of cackling laughter.

There was a drunk man, lying on one of the benches out the front of the supermarket. Shawn ignored him, pretending they weren't the same. The man said, "God bless you, sir. God bless," and then, "Stuck up arsehole," when Shawn didn't respond.

Shawn realized he looked stuck up because of the suit he was wearing, and liked that. He liked being in the skin of this man who had a girlfriend twenty years younger and the time and money to go breathe smoke for a weekend, forking over hundreds of dollars for the privilege. The cigarette the drunk smoked smelled like burned rubber. He was filthy. Barefoot. Covered with grime, his hair sticking out from so much dust. For a moment Shawn thought he was looking in a mirror but then he remembered he didn't look like that anymore. That was in the past. That was a long time ago, before he met his wife on the mountain top. Shawn relented, gave the man some coins, all he had in his pocket, then patted his wallet, making sure it was secure. He'd taken more money from the believers, because Moses hadn't left him any shopping money. He remembered now that Moses had told him not to bother, that they wouldn't be needing food, but that was nonsense. The kids would be starving; they at least would want pancakes. The air smelt dusty, burnt, because the day was hot. Too hot to be out. He smiled at a woman who glanced at him sideways.

He was used to this. Women found him handsome until they got up close and he was, once, charming and charismatic. Now he was skinny with hunched shoulders, but his eyes still clear blue. In his "borrowed" suit he felt taller, smarter, younger.

He mimicked turning off the gas stove to remind himself he'd done it. So much routine in his life it was hard to remember day-to-day even if he'd eaten.

He found his shopping list in the wallet and headed into the supermarket to buy what he needed. Then to the bottle shop, because his extra funds meant he could buy a case of beer if he wanted to.

He wanted to.

There was a cluster of people near the door, standing so close together they looked like they were intertwined. They moved toward him, all of their eyes on him. He hated being noticed like that, would prefer to be invisible like he usually was, so he turned and headed away from them.

The drunk man was swearing now, hurling abuse at people, and Shawn kept his distance. He didn't want to be there if the police came sniffing around. He didn't want them near his car, half-full of stuff that didn't belong to him, half-full of his own things. Not that he ever pinched anything worthwhile.

Shawn hadn't stolen anything of real value since he was a teenager, that famous camping trip when he'd raided the tents while the others chased the screams of a baby boy.

That was when he learned that distraction is the best way to succeed. No one ever noticed what he stole that night; the gold chain Gloria already thought she lost, money from Luke's wallet (he'd never notice), and the pointed compass they'd tattooed the girls with. He still had it, somewhere or other.

That evening, so many years ago, the five of them had hiked into the forest with four bottles of wine pinched from Shawn's foster parents, packs of cigarettes, ink, and the compass. Neil said they should get there early, set up before dark. They planned to stay out all night and he wanted shelter and the fire built.

This was a turning point for them all, the night they'd reject the lives their parents wanted for them, or at least detour into a different one for a while. The detour was minor and they all knew it, even at the time. Life wasn't black and white, failure and success. None of them planned to have a chaotic life.

Neil set the fire going and they unpacked the snacks that would do for dinner. They had forgotten cups so took turns drinking from the bottles. As always it was Shawn who had the lion's share, who wanted more than there was.

Shawn and Gloria sat close together but the others were just friends. None of them felt the need to hook up.

"What's the time?" Jane said. She yawned; she was always the first to go to sleep. The homemade tattoo on her forearm (*Uz 4 Eva*) had scabbed up, although she said it still throbbed. Shawn gave her the wine bottle again.

"It's only eleven," Luke said.

"You're kidding! It feels like about three a.m.," Jane said. She wrapped her arms around her knees.

"I'm busting," Shawn said. He shook his arse so they knew it was a shit rather than a piss he wanted. He headed off into the forest. It seemed much farther in the dark and he wished he'd brought a torch. Neil had tied a bright yellow t-shirt to a tree so they'd know which direction to head and where to avoid. Shawn dropped his shorts and squatted, holding the material out of the way.

So quiet. So peaceful. He could hear their voices. Not the words, but the reassuring hum of his friends talking, and over that a loud crack. He'd made that noise himself walking over here so he knew it was someone walking on a branch.

"Hang on, I'm nearly done," he said. He fixed himself up (no toilet paper) and headed to the campfire.

The others were all there so he didn't know which of them it was who'd spied on him, but he didn't ask as he approached because they were all staring at him.

Behind him.

He spun around and saw the woman. Tall, pale, her face bloodied, she held out her palms then pressed them together as if praying. She wore a hippy skirt and a loose top that was damp and stained.

She walked (limped; Shawn couldn't see her feet for blood) toward the fire then veered off to the side, turning once to pray at them.

"Wait, wait," Neil called. But she wouldn't wait, always tantalizingly ahead of them. How was she even moving? They couldn't see her feet but she seemed mangled, covered with blood.

Broken.

The others headed after her. Shawn was reluctant, not knowing where she'd lead them, and in the quiet, in the space they'd left him, he raided the tents for the necklace, watch, and compass. He hid them in his dirty socks then ran to catch up with his friends.

They followed the woman, walking for ten minutes or so until they heard a car idling.

"Is that my car? Fuck. Someone better not be trying to steal it," Luke said. It was his dad's car.

They walked on, jogging now, until a car's headlights glowed through the trees. And the sound of a baby crying weakly, and its voice cracked and raw, so they ran.

The driver's side door was open, and that woman was in there, slumped forward, both hands on the wheel. She'd crashed the car into a tree; the front was crumpled in, although the headlights still shone.

"Are you all right?" Gloria said. They crowded around her but there was no response. Her seatbelt was on and her feet were trapped under the dashboard. Neil reached over to undo her seatbelt, and he and Luke tried to pull her out but she was stuck.

Gloria and Jane went to the backseat, releasing a small baby from its car seat.

They had no idea how old, but the baby was tiny and red-faced, wet with sweat, its voice scratchy now as if it had been crying for a long, long time.

They somehow figured out how to get the baby out. Luke ran for his car, planning to drive to a phone. Neil continued trying to get the woman out but she was really stuck, her feet bloodied. She didn't regain consciousness before help arrived but all of them swore they saw a smile on her face.

They had nothing to give the baby but it stopped crying anyway as Shawn held it. "Gross," he said, because it was covered in shit, piss, sweat, but he didn't relinquish hold of it.

The baby heaved a sigh and Shawn felt such a wave of affection for it. Who would have thought this tiny thing would become Moses the smoke king, the sweat guru, the man who provided a roof and a job for Shawn? Not one of them would have guessed such a thing.

How did it feel, people later asked them. "Restful," Gloria said. "There was actually a sense of great peace."

"Tethered," Neil said, "like we have an unbreakable connection." Neil always spoke that way, in such lofty ideals. Most people thought it was teen hormones, mass hallucination, not real. The mother couldn't have led them to the car because she couldn't get out of the car. It was impossible.

As Shawn walked back to his car from the shops, the cluster of people came after him as if they knew who he was. His eyesight wasn't what it was so he couldn't see the faces reflected in shop windows; he glanced back, hoping to recognize them, to figure it out. They were all dressed in white and they seemed to shimmer in the heat.

They followed him, palms out, as he headed for his car, moving quickly in front of him, begging him to follow. He'd seen this before, from Moses's mother in the woods, and later when he climbed a mountain and saved the life of the woman who'd become his wife. The woman who'd made a deal with the devil he was still paying for.

The mountain had represented a challenge to him. On the day he rescued his wife, he reached the base of the staircase and paused. There were 252 steps to the top of this low mountain and he wanted to run them in one go, without stopping. He hadn't managed it yet, but today he felt fit and fine.

He had to pause for breath momentarily, glancing around to see if anyone was coming up behind him. Hill joggers could be so judgy. You could slow down but not stop. Pausing for breath made you a stroller, not a jogger. There was nobody else on the mountain, though, the reward of running on a Tuesday morning.

Fifty steps up, he swore. An old lady stopped up ahead, bent over the rust railings. She was in his way, her arse poking out. And she was tired or something; he'd have to help her.

The old him, the alcoholic dickhead, wouldn't have helped her. Wouldn't have been here, would have been stumbling around town, looking for coins, trying to smile at people, finding the $5 needed to buy a beer at the Labor Club. He was better now. Trying to be better. So he'd help.

When he neared he saw she wasn't so old, but that her legs were bent and buckled, bloodied. He jogged harder, then. He'd left his phone down in the car, an old habit, so if she was as badly hurt as she appeared he'd have to belt down the hill for help. He kept most of his belongings in the car; a car was harder to break into than his room. He'd tried feeding his housemates; like magpies, if you fed them, they got to know you, and maybe they wouldn't swoop you. But there was so much turn-over in the government flat he lived in you never knew who was going to be in the next room. Still, he cooked up a hot meal as often as he could. People were less bad-tempered with a full stomach.

"Hey, are you all right?" he called out, a stupid thing to say, but what else?

She stopped dragging herself and turned to look at him.

She was young, actually, early twenties at most, her face darkened down one side, the hair on the other side thick with blood.

As he neared her she sped up, dragged herself so quickly up the stairs he could only look on in shock as she disappeared over the edge.

Rust flaked off the railing as he raced up the stairs; this mountainside staircase needed repair.

At the top, he looked around. It was flattened up there, months of work for men with shovels and whatever else, tons of dirt carted down the mountain. One small table with bolted down chairs, and the power pole that justified the steps leading up. There was no sign of the woman.

His own breathing in his ear, the gentle rustle of leaves, the call of currawongs and noises in the grass overlaid a faint moaning.

On the other side of the mountain, he saw her about twenty meters down, her face in the dirt, her limbs laid over each other.

"Hey!" he called out as he stumbled down to her, grabbing long stalks of native grass for purchase, loose rubble making it precarious, and he turned his ankle briefly, causing a sharp but momentary flash of pain.

Her shadow seemed . . . lifted, until he stood beside her and watched as it nodded at him and then seemed to melt into itself, merging with the woman on the ground.

The woman groaned. He didn't need to take her pulse but did so, wanting to feel the life in her. He remembered the feel of baby Moses, when they rescued him, and Shawn held him, the coursing pulse of life in him, and wanted to feel it in this woman, too. He couldn't move her, not far at least and certainly not down the mountain.

He managed to turn her so she was face up. His t-shirt was wet with sweat and gross, so he cast around for something else for her to use as a pillow. He found an old wine bag, probably discarded by teenagers given that it was filled with air, and that would have to do. She smiled weakly and he smiled back. It was something. He touched her arm.

"Have you got a phone?" he asked, but clearly she didn't. She was dressed only in a hot pink singlet and a tiny skirt; there was no place for a phone. He looked briefly for a bag or backpack but saw nothing. He found something that looked a bit like yarrow, and he snatched up a handful to try to stem any bleeding.

She'd been there a while, though, and her wounds no longer bled.

"I'll go for help. I'll have to run down the hill. Here." He left his water bottle, half-full. "I won't be long."

She closed her eyes and he thought, *I've saved her life.*

Then he ran.

It took twelve minutes to reach his car and make the call, another seven for paramedics to arrive, then eighteen to get up the mountain. They were pretty fit but wearing uniforms and carrying equipment, so couldn't move as fast as he could. He ran ahead, and saw her there on the stairs again, dragging herself up torturously. "Wait," he said, "Let me help," but again she was gone by the time he reached her.

He waited at the top for the paramedics then pointed them down to where she lay.

"Jesus," one of them said, even though Shawn had already described her state as best he could.

The paramedics (a man and a woman, Shawn realized. It was hard to tell with the uniforms) stumbled down to her.

"She's still with us," the man said, and they worked to stabilize her, then unfolded a stretcher to carry her down.

"Given her condition," the woman said, "we'll have to get the coppers up here to investigate."

"I can help," Shawn said, but the look of utter distrust the paramedic woman gave him made him back off.

"Should I wait here for the cops?" he said, hoping to show his innocence this way.

"Yeah, keep people away from the area if you can," the bloke said. They'd radioed for police assistance. "They should be here soon."

Shawn jogged on the spot, starting to feel a chill in the air. He had maybe half an hour before darkness fell. He didn't want to be up here, then. Things changed at night. He was glad the girl was safe but didn't know what to do. Find her at the hospital? But he didn't even know her name and he hadn't given the paramedics his. He didn't have a business card that he could leave behind. He decided to call the police when he got home, so he could answer their questions, help in any way he could.

Still he stood at the top of the stairs, hoping the police would arrive soon, then back to look at the space where she'd been, then back to the stairs. He simply couldn't decide whether he should leave or not, so he sat at the top of the stairs and waited until dusk fell, and then made his way carefully down. No joggers or walkers passed him and he saw why at the bottom; the paramedics had dragged some fallen wood into the pathway, two pieces crossed over, to deter entry.

He half expected the police to be waiting for him. The news already had the story, calling him a Good Samaritan.

He arrived home at his government flat to find his door kicked in again. There was nothing in his room to steal except for his soap and a potted cactus, which they had tipped out, looking for drugs.

He thought, "I just saved a woman's life. I don't need this shit," and he climbed in his car and drove away.

He called the police to let them know who he was. He didn't want them to think badly of him, so lied, told them he was staying with his sister, although he hadn't seen her in years.

He'd long ago worn out his welcome there.

He didn't tell the police he'd seen the woman he'd saved climbing the stairs, leading him. That would confuse things and it seemed like nonsense now, unlikely. Impossible. Afterward he wasn't sure of the timeframe. Had he really seen her crisis apparition?

"Barely alive," is how she was described. He was *Good Samaritan* and she was *Woman Found Barely Alive*.

"Did she say anything?" the police asked him. They'd taken swabs of his hands and all the rest, checked his knuckles for damage. He could understand that, he really could, and he didn't resent it in the slightest. He wasn't charged.

"How did you know she was there? Hidden in the long grass?"

Here he was tempted to tell of her apparition, but he said, "I heard her singing. I think she was delirious at that point."

"Did you see anybody else?"

He'd seen nobody and she'd been there for an hour at least, probably more, when he found her.

The police said, "She'd like to see you." He wasn't too dirty but he went to the YMCA for a shower and to change into the clothes he'd got for free at the rubbish dump. He often found suits out there, and nice shirts. Once you gave them a wash, or hung them out to air clean at least, they were fine. On a warm day you'd hang them in your car and it was like ironing.

The police were pleased with him and what he'd done. That made a first, and he quite liked it.

He combed his hair and put on the walk, the confident stride he saw other men carry. He knew the hospital well; he'd spent enough time there.

She had a police officer sitting on the end of her bed because they didn't know who'd tried to kill her so they were taking no chances. Shawn was pleased they'd figured out it wasn't him.

She sat up in bed, her tray table full of grapes, books, chocolate. Last time he'd been in he didn't get any visitors but he wouldn't have wanted them, not with him in that state. He cringed now to think of himself, how bad tempered, how deluded, he'd been. He'd refused to wash, just to be an arsehole.

"G'day love," he said. "How are you?"

"I'm actually pretty good," she said. She spoke quietly, her voice scratchy.

"She's a trooper," the police officer said. Shawn didn't know what to say, so he asked her name.

"Rhonda. And you're Shawn, aren't you? I tried so hard, Shawn. I searched so many times."

"We've been asking how she got there. Who did this to her," the officer said.

Shawn felt suddenly, violently protective.

"Can you remember? Was it a stranger or someone you know?"

"I've never been good at picking boyfriends."

"Is that who it was?"

She closed her eyes. The police officer put her hand on Shawn's shoulder to hold him down, and she was right, he was rising to run in the street and find this man, as ridiculous as this was.

The girl was about twenty-five, ten years younger than him.

"We'll sort it," the police officer said, and she stood in the doorway to mutter into her radio. (Later they caught her boyfriend. He'd show up on the TV, saying, "She shouldn't be alive. She's done a deal with the devil. You better figure out what she's offered."

Shawn would come to think the same thing.)

After, when it was just them, he told Rhonda about his teenage camping trip and how that mother had saved her baby's life. He didn't confess that he had been stealing from his friends while the others followed her to the car.

"But she died?" Rhonda said.

"She did, but she knew she'd saved her baby at least. She didn't die before she knew that." Shawn wasn't sure of this but it sounded good. "And she got him away from his father, who's still in jail, I think. Brought up by his grandparents. We keep track of him."

Rhonda's eyes were wide; his story entranced her so he went on with it.

"You should see him. He's all about fate and healing and faith. He's looking for meaning, for the message, for the sense of it."

"I'd been up and down those steps four times. I couldn't get any farther than halfway, found myself turned around and walking back up again. And I was so tired, when you found me. I had to have faith. I did. I was so tired."

"Beautiful and tired," he said. It occurred to him that they had described Moses's mother in the same way.

If they'd been different people they would have sought publicity.

Shawn's life had changed. Before, every day had been a struggle uphill, to keep away from the booze, the bad influences. The way of his drinker friends was so easy, so much fun. It required nothing of him but enough money to buy alcohol and the occasional burger to keep himself alive. But that wasn't enough and he knew it. Simple survival wasn't enough. It had been a struggle, every day, with only himself to care, his own face in the mirror.

But now? Knowing that he wouldn't have saved Rhonda's life if he'd been drunk? That helped. He felt tethered. Secure.

Once she was recovering at home he visited often. She lived with her aunt and two cousins, all of them busy. Loving but busy. Rhonda would wait for his visits.

The police had asked her to try to remember who bashed her, how she got to the mountain, so together they pretended they were there. He brought her things from the mountain top. Fern leaves, stones, torn notes, flowers. Before long she'd be well enough to climb, and they'd go together. It was the place they met, after all. The place Shawn became a hero.

And they married.

And it was good until it fell apart.

She invited all of his friends from the past to the wedding, and his sister, and his father. His teen friends had stayed in touch with each other, not so much with him. All of them protective of Moses, supportive, with Neil in particular ensuring his financial future was secure.

There had been five but Luke died in a car crash. He always

said he would, said every time he got in the car the ghost of Moses's mother sat in the back urging him to go faster, speed up, save her baby. ("I keep telling her we did but she doesn't believe me," Luke would say). The ghost distracting him, but still he drove.

Besides Shawn, there was Gloria, Jane, and Neil left. He never saw them again, after the wedding. There'd been some kind of shit fight. He didn't remember what it was about; he'd had a lapse, all that champagne. All that booze. Neil swanned about showing off his money. He was managing director of something or other, Shawn didn't care enough to remember. Neil paid for group holidays that Shawn didn't get to go on.

The best, if short-lived, thing to come out of the marriage was reconciliation with his sister, but he lost that, too. The two women became so close that they squeezed him out. Made him irrelevant. This still hurt. This made him vulnerable and needy when he hated being both of those things.

Rhonda tried to reconcile him with his father but the last time he'd seen his father he'd babbled like an idiot, on and on, filling the spaces because he didn't want to hear what his father had to say.

Things went well until they didn't. He could barely remember now how it went wrong and he understood, at least, that was the problem.

They knew it was over when Shawn raised his hand to Rhonda when she asked him about their drained bank account. She recoiled, covering her eyes, her face, shrinking from him as if he were a demon.

"I'm not going to hit you," he said, his voice almost a whisper. He blamed her for his drinking. Hadn't he been off it before? Hadn't he climbed mountains and saved her life? He felt like she was bright and new, and he was old and stiff. Things went well until he realized that she'd only married him out of gratitude and a belief in fate. He repeated what her ex-boyfriend had said on

TV—the one who'd try to kill her—that she'd done a deal with the devil. It made sense to him now, in his anger, that she must have sent her soul out looking for him and that she was empty now, soulless.

"I'm soulless?" she said. Her voice was quiet too; they never shouted.

He didn't see her ghost those months later; she didn't come to him. The irony wasn't lost on anybody who knew them, that she was the one who died driving drunk. She did appear to his sister, though, who called him and said, "Is she all right?" and he told his sister Rhonda had left him and he didn't know where she was or if she was all right but she wasn't. Rhonda had said to him, *you didn't save my life for this*, as if he'd failed her badly, and that hurt.

He felt a sense of release at her death. Relief. An untethering that set him free.

He reached his car now and opened up the back door to store the shopping. There were people inside there, though, two children dressed in white and two old people, all of them reaching for him. He backed away, tripping over the curb and landing hard on his arse, and they were around him then, as if they could help him up. "Fuck off!" he shouted, waving his arms as if shooing flies or buzzing insects. He needed a drink so opened a bottle and skulled it on the spot, sitting there in the gutter. He didn't care. If he drank enough they might leave him alone.

He needed more.

Heading back to the bottle shop, he saw that someone had wheeled an old piano into the courtyard by the library, hoping to liven up the dull shopping precinct. They'd painted it with flowers, and the words *play me*. Wearing the borrowed suit, in this assumed identity, Shawn felt as if he would be able to play. That he could sit at the seat and make beautiful music. If he looked like himself no one would take him seriously for a second, but as he approached the piano people—not just the ones dressed in white—began to gather. An attractive woman bent over the keys, looking at him sidelong as if asking him for a song. He thought that if he could play she would stand close, put her hand on his shoulder and ask him to perform some kind of love song. Another, whose high ponytail made her look a bit like his late wife, stretched her fingers out at him.

"Go on, mate," the drunk from the supermarket who'd abused him said, "give us a tune," and for a moment, Shawn thought he could. He sat down, contemplating the keys. There was a crackling, like someone opening a packet of chips at the theatre, and he *shshshshshed* loudly, making a joke, hoping for a laugh. A crowd gathered but they were odd, all of them, dank in smell and opaque, like looking through smoky glass. One appeared to have burns on one side; she was almost naked but seemed barely bothered. He thought she was familiar, perhaps one of the parade of people who came to the building for help. He didn't look too hard at any of them, standing too close and pressing him, some of them with palms out prayerfully. He sat at the piano and the crowd closed in. He took a deep breath, as if waiting for something magical to happen. As if he would be able to play.

He couldn't. It didn't. He plunked, as anyone who can't play the piano will do. He was the same with the guitar, useless, although he'd buy them from the second hand shop all the time, every time someone pinched one.

"Sorry, folks," he said, but no one laughed or even responded. He plunked some notes but that didn't scare them off. More of them appeared around the piano. In front. Behind. Then more of them, coming at him.

His pink shoes looked ridiculous on the piano pedals.

He felt compelled to head for home so stood up from the piano. They followed him, appearing and reappearing like his wife on the mountain and he walked faster. They coughed dramatically, choking, and he thought: *People aren't meant to breathe smoke.*

Now beside him, closer, and one of them was Moses, falling to his knees and shaking his head.

Moses was always on about being rescued as a baby, but he wasn't the one paying the price, was he? He was such a gentle man, such an angel, people said with his curly hair, his perfect teeth. What would his life have been with that woman, that mother of his, deserting his father so recklessly?

"Mate?" Shawn said, and he reached out to put his hand on Moses's shoulder, because for all the curses, for all that everybody else who'd rescued Moses was dead, Moses had provided a home and a job for him. Shawn's hand slid through him and it was then (and he knew how slow he'd been, how stupid) that he realized the believers had come to him for help and that Moses believed they should be left where they were, that Shawn should leave them alone.

When they found Moses as a baby, he'd cried so long his vocal chords were damaged. Never spoke well again. He always spoke softly. Like Rhonda, he had felt much pressure to live a good life. To make the most of it. After what he'd said of Rhonda, Shawn had begun to think the same of Moses, to blame him, that they'd both made a deal with the devil, deliberate or not. People had looked after Moses his entire life. He'd had it easy. But he talked about the curse of having your life saved. "You can never forget. You're always being reminded that you need to achieve. You need to make something of yourself."

"What about me? What about having saved a life? Having saved two?"

"There is an obligation on you," Moses had said. Shawn knew

how disappointed he was to have Shawn the only one of his rescuers left. Because the others were all dead now. They had all felt blessed. Not worthy, but blessed, as if Moses had come into their lives to give them worth. Shawn saw the opposite. A curse, this tethering, something that held him back and filled him with guilt. The girls, Jane and Gloria, had died together after going overseas for beauty treatment. Neil said, "I would have paid. I would have given them the money." At the funeral Shawn saw that both of them had scars on their arms, removal of the tattoos they'd done so many years ago.

Neil had drowned in a spa.

Shawn sometimes wondered if he was next, if the curse would land on him. He wasn't ready to die. He needed redemption first. He needed to better himself. He couldn't die this man. But now wasn't the time to change either. He wasn't ready. Not yet.

He had to wait until he was ready.

The smell of smoke was stronger back at the house. He made himself a coffee on the gas stovetop, adding a good splash of rum to the cup, then moved from room to room, opening doors to allow a breeze to move through. There was temptation everywhere, from the smallest bedroom that he thought belonged to twin teens, eighteen he thought they were. He scored more money from them and a stash of miniature booze bottles which he drank on the spot. Sunglasses. Two cameras, lots of photos that were worthless but fascinating, the two of them dressed alike in every one. Other rooms yielded women's handbags and these were the best, filled with treasure. Secret items and notebooks, money, dice, all sorts of things. He had a garbage bag with him to chuck it all in but he hesitated. He couldn't come back if he took all this. It'd be done.

"It's your fault," Moses liked to say to people. "You have to stop blaming other people." Shawn's wife used to say this to him, too, but he didn't know which of them came up with it first.

Moses had said, "You are responsible for the people you save and they will stay with you for all eternity. Similarly, those you choose to die with, those who accept the word, will also be with you, but will be there to hear your word into all eternity. This is how fate lays things out for us. That's what you call Heaven."

He told Shawn, "You blame your wife for doing a deal with the devil and you saved her because of it. No. There was no deal involved; there is just fate, and the way we follow it will lay our lives out for us."

Shawn felt the slightest twinge of guilt as he searched the family's room but they should have learned the lesson about keeping your stuff safe. Leave it lying around, it gets pinched; basic fact of life. He knocked over a vase of flowers but felt too dizzy to clean it up.

He nodded a greeting to the young girl slumped against the wall (he wanted to slump with her, weariness overwhelming him) and she reached out to him. That wasn't his business, though. Not his department. He hoped she couldn't see into the garbage bags he carried, and wondered what he'd stolen from her. She was the one fucking the rich older guy, he thought, so it was the earrings and the perfume. He squinted at her to see if she was wearing a necklace but she seemed to fade into the gloom.

There were people on the stairs, dragging themselves up and Shawn felt for his car keys and hoped he could drive. His fingers felt numb but he wasn't numb enough so he finished the rum in the bottle he carried with him. He nodded at them and they held their palms out to him, a young girl of about thirteen, a little boy tugging at her jeans. And a really skinny woman, so skinny he wondered how her legs didn't break. The old couple, Mr. and Mrs. Minter, crouched down at the bottom, but he thought maybe they were begging him to leave them be, let them go. If he was that old, that decrepit, he wouldn't want to live for a long time either.

He tried the basement door and listened, but then Moses was beside him, shaking his head *no*. Moses pointed up the stairs, then shook his fingers as if to say *go now. You're free.*

They followed him up the stairs and out to the car as if he were the Pied Piper leading away the souls, the crisis apparitions.

And he kept driving with them crowded in the car with him, as one by one they disappeared until the last of them went and it was finally too late for him to save anyone.

CRISIS APPARITION:
A COMMENTARY

OUR FLAWED PROTAGONIST IN "CRISIS APPARITION"
—bound and then ultimately released by the cult leader he once
rescued—is a good Samaritan gone bad, haunted by ghosts of a
particular kind.

A "crisis apparition" is the spirit of one very near death (in
"crisis"), their body *in extremis*, soul separating from the mortal
coil right before the final act. Although Shawn stumbles
accidentally into his encounters with these desperate spirits, his
ability seals him into a fate that is dependent on them. He is a
reluctant kind of hero, and over the course of the story we learn
that his selfish and petty ways—from stealing frivolous items from
his friends to marrying a woman he saves for questionable
reasons—undermines his ability to recognize how these spirits
might be helping him, as well.

Unlike Ebenezer Scrooge from Dickens's *A Christmas Carol,*

Shawn does not learn from his visitations, and earns the fate that is in store for him in the story's chilling but ultimately necessary conclusion. In fact, he is more akin to Dickens's protagonist in "The Signal Man," who should have seen his own future foreshadowed by these ghosts who persistently reach out to him.

—Michael Arnzen, PhD

WHY KAARON WARREN MATTERS

BY MICHAEL ARNZEN, PHD

WHEN LOOKING ACROSS THE ARTFUL SHORT
fiction of Kaaron Warren, one can't help but notice that her work is
diverse in its approach, rich in its prose style, and stunning in its
character-driven plotting. The stories feel very real, even when they
delve into the most imaginary of realms, and when she's not just
making it all up on her own, you feel a sense of authenticity and
truth grounded in both research and cultural legend. She is true to
the heart of her characters, faithful to the complexity of their desire.
Kaaron Warren matters because her writing is populated by ghosts
that reveal through their power the flaws and frailties of our culture.
She is a very mindful writer, speaking through her phantoms and
specters on behalf of those that a culture historically silences, giving
them voice or showing their courage in the face of oppression.
There is a feminist impulse in her work that is refreshing for a genre
still dominated today by male authors and male audiences; she
resists adapting the templates of the past without challenging what
they take for granted, resulting in fresh original writing with
something new to teach us about what we thought we already knew.

I do not know if Kaaron Warren would identify herself as a feminist writer, *per se*, but she matters because she delves into gender issues as a whole with finesse and complexity and her work can never be reduced to the level of preaching or espousing dogma. She recognizes, I wager, that all mankind is othered and marginalized by the indifference of the universe, and that horror fiction is a great equalizer in that regard. Perhaps that's why she is attracted to such dark material: because it is both liberating to the imagination as well as allowing writers the freedom to explore alternatives to the way things are (the *status quo*) unlike any other genre. But she also seems to know that there's no room for petty hierarchies, sexual violence, and related patriarchal nonsense in a universe larger and stronger than all mankind, so she critiques such ideologies through her work.

Ghosts, in my view, dominate Warren's writing—she is engaging in what some critics would call "hauntology." When ghosts aren't present overtly as archetypal figures, her main characters still remain haunted by something they wish to avoid, something repressed in their everyday life. These ghosts are not merely phantom menaces who spook intruders. They are spirits liberated from their bodies, abstractions made real in the ether, revenants who haunt a place until a justice can be served. Revenant stories are typical of the haunted house genre, where visitors or new occupants are essentially stalked by some evil spirit. But Warren's fiction is usually more interested in the ghosts than the people that they spook, and this is evident in the point of view she chooses to tell their tales. Hers are not just ghost stories—they are the *ghosts'* stories. She is not just telling tall tales about bringing a criminal to justice; these are *social justices* that her revenants demand, and the uncanny elements of her fiction bring culture's secret injustices from everyday life sharply into the light.

One of my favorites in the present collection that perfectly illustrates why Warren matters is the tight flash fiction story, "The Wrong Seat." On one level it seems a simple ghost story, depicting a woman who dies on a bus and whose spirit seems damned to haunt that space, as well as the depot when it arrives. Over and over, the cycle of the bus route continues, with many of the same passengers who first ignored her when she was stabbed by a random man on the bus and ignored by the other passengers as she bled to death. In a typical ghost story, the murderer who slashed this innocent woman's throat would somehow be unmasked or avenged, or the ghost would get its revenge on her killer by haunting or attacking him from the spirit world.

But such is not the case with Moira Braddon. She is introduced as too timid and shy for such vengeful tactics. The very title, "The Wrong Seat," suggests she was an innocent victim of circumstances, sitting in the wrong place at the wrong time. And there is a mild degree to which this is true, because the attack on her seems to be a random hit by a throat-slashing maniac, who sneaks up on her and then escapes without a trace. But Warren does not merely make her some dupe of fate; the entire characterization of Moira is scripted to call attention to her kindness and moral propriety. She's in the wrong seat, after all, because she gave her own ticketed seat up to another passenger, a bull of a man who mostly avoids conversing with her, so he can stare at his own reflection in the bus window. She is kind to him anyway, and also kind enough to another man who she pursued in a "failed attempt at romance" by showing up at his doorstep uninvited, which accounts for her travelling on the bus to begin with. Her kindness is exploited by these men, who take it for granted. Even the killer exploits her niceties when he leans over and slits her throat, because she offered it up with closed eyes, thinking he was about to kiss her.

Clearly, we are led to see Moira as an innocent victim of men, since the cruel worldviews of such men allow them to ignore, mislead, or exploit "nice girls" and helpless romantics like our ghostly protagonist. But Warren is not merely male-bashing here, because the story resists any urge to simply attack these culprits with ghostly revenge. Instead, Warren stays with Moira's frustrations trying to understand her situation, progressively testing out her new identity as a ghost. What happens in the process is an allegory for the movement from passive acceptance of her female identity as it is constructed by men toward mastery over her status as autonomous woman—literally a "free" spirit, despite her purgatorial imprisonment in mass transit.

Moira is stuck in a cycle, but she learns to see the patterns that hold her back as they repeat. Her exploration of her powers is as comedic as it is transgressive. She is a kind ghost but grows progressively frustrated with the lack of communication between herself and these outsiders from the "real" world. She studies them, sits on their laps, spies on their conversations, and eventually rides the bully who stole her seat on piggyback. Interestingly, her ghostly ectoplasm does manage to connect with the bus passengers but only as a smell, and this odor is not merely one of decay, but one described as abject. This is not mere juvenile gross-out humor; there is a subtle way in which Warren is using the repulsive as a form of power.

Abjection—the repulsive body, here in the ghostly form of the smell of decay—is a reminder to civilized culture that the body is never as proper and civilized and controlled as it would like it to be. Scholars following Julia Kristeva's theories of abjection outlined in her book *The Powers of Horror* (feminists like Barbara Creed in her study of *The Monstrous Feminine*) have shown how women's bodies often are aligned with abjection because patriarchal culture sees them as both "lesser" than the physical power of the male body, while also demanding that it remain "pure" for male pleasure and to produce proper offspring. In Warren's story, "She grew to need those looks of disgust," that her ghost-smell generates among the people, "because they meant she existed." Moira *owns her abjection* and uses it as a form of communication and manipulation over the patriarchal passengers.

Moira takes charge of her situation, embraces her freedom—even her smelliness—in order to exist. She exists more powerfully as a ghost than she did as a "nice girl." And her mastery over this newfound role becomes a metaphor for *empowerment*. In the story's conclusion, she virtually chases the bully who took her seat off the bus with her odor—by refusing to allow him to escape it—and in the process he is thrown from the bus and dies by hitting his head against a pole. While she is not directly responsible for his death, the accident is enough to change the power relationship between them. This is why she utters "Enough" after looking at him. She's done pursuing him. She's done playing the role of the subordinate woman, the opposite "pole" to dominant masculinity, which is ultimately self-destructive. And this is why the tables turn and "she left, before he could rise and give chase." Warren leaves it open-ended: does she just leave the scene of the accident, of her "crime," or does she leave the bus terminal altogether now that she's had "enough"? Will the man "give chase" to finally pursue her romantically, or is it to just take over her role giving chase to everyone else? It is unclear, but one thing is for certain: Moira has changed, and Moira has left behind her old self, as well as the system that has oppressed her, symbolized by the dead male.

I have deconstructed "The Wrong Seat" to illuminate just how much significance Kaaron Warren can pack into a very short story, by siding the reader's interest with the ghosts of her fiction, allowing us to witness the viewpoint of those who are alienated but struggling, outsiders but autonomous, marginalized but seeking empowerment through their best efforts. Warren matters because she says that *everyone* matters.

Look at the protagonists of some of the other works of fiction in this collection and you'll see that they often are women who grapple with the situations that have been handed to them by an oppressive culture. In "Sins of the Ancestors"—the most science-fictional story gathered here—a prostitute plays to the death fantasies of rich men who abuse and spit on her as an abject body to loathe for her very subordination to fulfilling their wishes for profit. She manipulates her circumstances to seek escape with her brother, in a gambit to clear her family name so they can travel. She ends up a victim of her own lineage—sent to death for the sins of an uncle (the patrilineage) by the dominant male forces in her culture. It is a tragic ending. But there is a smattering of hope in the story's conclusion, because she did all she could in an admirable way, at least achieving some kind of freedom in the "dream death" fantasy of the final passage of the story. In "Born and Bread," a woman masters her doughy body in order to become a baker who saves the village from a grotesque male lech, turning his lust from beyond-the-grave against him. The women in Warren's stories often are haunted by the lusting, power-hungry men in their worlds, but when these women come to grips with the abject status that patriarchy gives them, and take mastery over their bodies and identities, they find strength and power.

Likewise, when Warren dramatizes male characters in these stories, they often are haunted by women they have wronged, or their own repressed dark wishes, which uncannily return to them as spectral forces that they cannot escape. In "Guarding the Mound," a young man achieves his "manhood" by keeping guard over the resting place of a tribal chieftain—quite literally, he becomes a man by protecting male-domination. The guarding of patriarchal rule even beyond the grave leads to utter ruin, in a realm where the chieftain keeps his power, but in an isolated and lonely and ultimately meaningless existence, detached from the community this power ostensibly keeps in place. It is strongly implied in this social allegory that holding on too tightly to outdated, male-dominated cultural systems can only lead to destruction even as it tries to protect a legacy. Similarly, in "Crisis Apparition," the protagonist is stuck in his role as "Good Samaritan," and can only escape by turning his back on both the wife he used and the child he saves from a car wreck (almost as if he has become its father, its guardian)—ultimately abandoning his community—strange and perhaps sick as it is—like a deadbeat dad, leaving for the great beyond in the final passages of the tale. Here the cult in the sweat lodge implicitly too becomes a collective of ghosts, of the dead which he is partially responsible for, and which he abandons for his own selfish pursuits, only to lose his life and meet his fate after all. In other words, these male protagonists get what they seek at the cost of severing all human relations and are relegated to as much alienation from society as Moira from "The Wrong Seat"—only their fate is cursed and they are disempowered in the process.

If there is any escape from this conservative impulse to "hold on" to a cultural past or to withdraw into the antisocial privileges of patriarchy, it's given in "Death's Door Café," where a man gets a "second chance" at life, which requires rejecting all the symbols of success (such as wealth and women) in order to start again and live a more meaningful human existence. He is a good man but wishes to be a better one; he seeks love, family, and a new life—positive human relations. Yet he also never quite forgets the damage that can happen when a collective group is treated with violence, as symbolized by the massacre of bats that haunts him in his second life. Stories, ghost lives, are what ensure that we never forget the sins of the past.

All said, what is "haunting" about Warren's ghosts is very different than those of pulp era horror literature. Her ghosts are not some ancient undead spirit seeking revenge, but some present and hidden power structure that mists through the cracks of reality and insists upon change. Often these changes are *compelled* by storytelling. Kaaron Warren matters because her stories portray the need for social justice in a dark world where injustice is taken for granted, and she does so in a way that entertains through dark fantasy and thereby triggers a sense of wonder about how things might be different if we were more willing to communicate, more willing to listen, to the voices of the silenced.

They might be sitting right next to us this very moment, even.

In Conversation with Kaaron Warren

ERIC J. GUIGNARD: Hi Kaaron, and it's great to chat with you. Thanks again for being part of this project! To start with, "Guarding the Mound" is one of my favorite stories by you. It starts off so simply, and then unexpectedly grows to this epic fantasy of descendancy, memory, and, ultimately, oblivion, for truly nothing lasts forever. I've always loved epic stories such as this, narratives that cross boundaries of time, ideas that encompass both the past and the future. You seem to have no difficulty crossing genres and time places—whether historical, present day, near-future, far-future, etc. Do you prefer writing in eras you have not experienced or do you favor grounding your characters and situations in relatable circumstances? Is it easier or harder to use an imaginary setting or era rather than a "real" one, and/or is there more meaning to do so?

KAARON WARREN: I'm so pleased you like this story. It is one of the few that came to me in a flash, fully formed. My kids were really young at the time (maybe three and one?) so my writing time was very limited. I remember writing part of this standing at the stove cooking Bolognese sauce! Stirring with one hand, writing with the other!

I enjoy both writing in eras I haven't experienced and writing in the present. I think the key part of your question here is 'relatable circumstances.' No matter what era or place you're writing in, you have to make that situation relatable in one way or another. Mostly this is by connecting the reader to the characters, so that the character experience becomes the reader's. In *Frankenstein*, for example, Victor Frankenstein is repulsed by the "monster" he has created. This is mostly seen as an element of character reveal, but I also think it is a story-telling trick; if he is repulsed then so are we. If Victor isn't repulsed, then the description changes and our first exposure to the Creature changes.

Even when using a so-called non-imaginary setting, I am making lots of creative choices and changes. It's easier in many ways, because you can twist the setting to suit your story. But, as the German writer Dirk Kurbjuweit says, "It's harder in others because fiction needs to make more sense than non-fiction does." In real life, ridiculous coincidences happen all the time. Strange meetings and odd occurrences. In fiction, you have to make sense of all of that. You don't get away with "it just happened." The same with the settings; they have to make sense in a fictional sense, and each thing you describe needs to have a place in the story, or at least in the world-building.

I don't know if there is more meaning in an imaginary setting. Certainly there is more of a imprint of the author in that scenario. And the creation of your own setting means you can layer it in meaning and symbolism. But I think you can do that in a "real" setting as well, with choice of words and descriptions.

EJG: If you could have the world read one piece of your fiction, what would it be?

KW: This is a terrible question, Eric! How can you make me choose just one? I refuse to answer!

The novels are all different but I'm proud of all of them and would happily read each if I hadn't written them. I hate rereading my own novels once they're out but you kinda have to because you forget details that people ask you about! *The Grief Hole* is my most recent novel and one people seem to like.

My short stories... you've actually chosen some of my own favorites, including "Guarding the Mound" and "The Wrong Seat." The stories that people most think of are "Dead Sea Fruit" and "All You Can Do is Breathe."

EJG: You wrote an original story for this Primer book, "Crisis Apparition," exploring the paranormal phenomenon of individuals in dire trauma being able to project a vision of themselves to others in order to deliver a final message or entreaty for help. There are many reports in the news today of eyewitness accounts to this experience, and beliefs suggest a number of reasons, such as it being an analogy or likeness of guardian angels, or a telepathic link to those with whom senders share the strongest relationships. Interestingly, Crisis Apparitions are considered the most reported type of "ghost" sightings. Do you believe that ghosts—in any form—may have the ability to make contact with the living, even if for only the briefest of time?

KW: I really, really want to believe this because it would prove the existence of the soul and therefore of an afterlife. Regardless of what that afterlife is, the idea that life ends here . . . is terrifying.

In my fiction I explore many variations of the possibility of ghosts. "Crisis Apparition" is one of the explorations where, as you say,

I'm looking at the idea that a person near death can send out an apparition seeking help. In all of the reportings of these apparitions, I'm not sure how many are successful in saving the person. Sightings of crisis apparitions are perhaps wishful thinking, they are "if onlys."

EJG: We all have pitfalls or bouts of writer's block or creative doubts or insecurities. What is your writing Kryptonite?

KW: Oh, gosh. Definitely imposter's syndrome, and the idea that I'm only as good as my last story and the next one is utter crap and unreadable. I'm never quite convinced that I've done the best by a story until I've sold it to an editor!

One of the things I find the hardest is finding the right voice for a story. Each voice delivers a different story and directs the way the story unfolds. Often I'll write it three or four different ways, until I find that right voice. Finding it is the magic, though! Once the voice emerges, the story flows.

EJG: One of the most emotionally-wrecking stories I've ever read was "All You Can Do is Breathe," which you wrote for an Ellen Datlow anthology in 2011. In the story, a miner is trapped underground for seven days; eventually he's rescued, while his coworker dies. It's purely by luck that he should have survived, yet credit seems also due to his cheery optimism. He's hailed a hero for his resolve, his sort-of "blue-collar idealism." But then a cold apparition drains him of that very certitude, of all his joy. Physically he's the same, but emotionally, he's been suffocated. His fate, it seems, is almost worse than death, the inability to feel anything, while then becoming resented by those who once lauded him, yet none knowing why he's changed. Personally this is one of the worst things I can imagine, that sense of becoming disdained by those around you, or losing any "meaning in life." Was this story written on a personal note or fear? How much control do you think we actually have over our own lives, over our dispositions, when we're constantly influenced by our surroundings, our environment, or other "unknowns," which we have so little control of?

KW: One of my starting points in writing a story I've designated as horror is to identify what fear I want to explore. I'll often write the words "fate worse than death!" So you've picked up on that brilliantly. This is exactly what I tried to capture.

The story was inspired by two different rescues in Australia, and a comment made by Henry Rollins, whom I saw live in spoken-word concert a number of years ago. He was inspired by a man called Stuart Diver, who survived the Thredbo Landslide. Diver was trapped in his bed (I think), with his wife dead beside him and water rising and falling to cover his face. He survived by lifting himself up on his elbows out of the water. He did this for days (I'd have look up the details to be sure how many) before he was finally rescued. Rollins said of him, and I'm paraphrasing, *if only we could open up his veins and bottle what he has. That instinct to survive.* I remember Rollins holding out both arms to us, underside of wrists facing up.

The other rescue was the Beaconsfield Disaster, a mine collapse in Tasmania. Two men, Todd Russell and Brant Webb, spent more than three hundred hours undergrounds. As they emerged at last, they "clocked out," a joke they must have planned and that demonstrated such spirit. I saw one of them at a local club a few months later, surrounded by people who just wanted to touch him, as if he could share some that magic, that survival magic, with them. He was very gracious, signing autographs and smiling, but I had my vision of people being like vampires, wanting to suck his blood. There is the media, of course, also wanting stories from the Beaconsfield survivors and of Stuart Diver, and that informed the story, too.

This has motivated elements of the story "Crisis Apparition," too. Whereby a survivor is expected to lead a good life, to achieve more than the ordinary person, to be grateful for the rest of their live. As to how much control we have over our lives, with all the influences you name, all you can do is control the way you respond to these things. You can control the way you treat other people, and how you respond to the influences.

EJG: I found it fascinating to read in your autobiographical account of your experiences growing up in a Hare Krishna family and your involvement with other spiritual movements while in childhood; it was a poignant moment to imagine you as a girl writing to friends telling of a "different" life. Knowing that you began writing stories sometimes as escapism from that, and that our childhood molds who we are, do you think if you were raised in a more conventional household, you would still have developed such a deep passion for writing? I suppose it's a lot of "what if" situations that make us who we are today, but if you could go back and change parts of your childhood, would you?

KW: I would definitely still be a writer. My dad was, still is, a voracious reader and whatever the circumstance always had books available. A lot of science fiction, so I was reading Nebula award anthologies and that sort of thing from a very young age. This sort of reading made me realize that anything is possible. I read fairy tales and all the kids' books available at the time. I was often disappointed in the endings, finding them either too predictable or trite and unnecessarily "tied up." So I'd imagine my own endings.

Beyond that, I have this thing that perhaps a lot of writers have, where words form themselves into stories. I often say that even a spelling list, like the ones we were given in primary school, form a story. An index forms a story, a dictionary, three headlines on a page. I see the words separately but also together.

So I can't really imagine what sort of life would have made me feel differently about words, reading, and writing them.

I wouldn't change my childhood. The overriding feeling I have, the sense that I have looking back, is of being loved, and nobody can really ask for more than that. For a long time I wished that I was more ordinary, but you realize that no one is. Everyone has their stories and secrets and no one thinks they are ordinary.

EJG: What does "Success as a Writer" look like to you?

KW: The answer to this one changes by the day! If ever I feel as if I haven't succeeded, as if my dreams haven't come true, I look at the bookcase carrying my novels and collections and all the anthologies and magazines carrying my stories. *I DID IT*. I used to sign birthday cards "From Karen Warren, Famous Writer" (hadn't changed the spelling of my name back then!). It was always what I wanted to do, who I wanted to be. I wanted to be published, to have readers, so journaling was never enough for me. I wanted an audience! A family friend gave me a list of possible markets when I was about fourteen. She was the first one to say, "this is what you need to do if you're taking this seriously."

BUT you have to keep striving. Shifting the goal posts, aiming higher. I want to be a better writer, so I read, write, practice. Write, rewrite, edit, discard, write again. I want to be the sort of writer I imagined I'd be when I was seven.

EJG: I read in another interview of you that one of your favorite things to read are "weird specialist magazines." This sounds intriguing! Tell us a bit more what this means, and which ones are most recommended.

KW: This is one of my weird obsessions. I buy these magazines second-hand, at yard sales or thrift stores (in Australia we'd say garage sales and op shops!). I like them because of the details in them, and because they are full of assumed knowledge. All of them have people who are famous within the realms of the world they describe (from 4WD drivers to poultry farmers, from lawyers to advertising people) and who are completely unknown outside that world. I love the magazines because of the insight they give me into other people's obsessions and occupations. Some memorable ones include the following:

University of Cambridge Magazine, CAM. The issue I have carries a story about what students have for breakfast, and a "then and now" story about people occupying the same dorm room over the decades.

Australasian Poultry talks about "myths about cleaning," although as far as I could tell there were no myths discussed, let alone ones needing debunking. Another talks about the "lifetime experience" of attending the World Poultry Congress, which sets my story-telling brain off in so many different ways.

Fire Journal (January 1977) has articles about putting out hospital fires and facts about sporting ammunitions fires. There's a whole section of fires and how they were dealt with, including listing the fatalities. The language used is different from that used in a newspaper, for example. "The employee opened a discharge valve on the tank in order to steam purge it." This is the sort of detail I'm talking about. Specific language that makes sense to a specific group of people, less so to others.

I also love *Man, Myth and Magic*, which is full of stories of ghosts, rituals, sacrifices, and all sorts. Fabulous pictures in that one!

I'm thinking of writing a novel inspired in part by these magazines. More on that soon!

EJG: In the spirit of Mad Libs, please select one of each:

   i. PRESENT TENSE VERB
   ii. EMOTION
   iii. ADJECTIVE
   iv. NOUN

Now answer this question:

When Kaaron *<insert Present Tense Verb>*, she is *<insert emotion>* as a *<insert adjective> <insert noun>*. Have you always been like this, and do you wish otherwise?

KW: With my fill-ins, it's this:

When Kaaron *DRIVES,* she is *TERRIFIED* as an *ENGORGED BRAIN.*

This is funny! I don't like driving much and am indeed a tiny bit terrified of the road. So, yes, I wish it was otherwise. I should do one of those defensive driving courses, shouldn't I?

EJG: What does the future hold for Kaaron Warren's writing career?

KW: I have a novel coming out from Omnium Gatherum in 2018, am nearly finished writing the next, and have ideas for about four more.

Lots and lots of short story ideas, so hopefully lots of those too.

I'm hoping to attend as many conventions and conferences as I can. I'd love to get to ICFA one year. I'm Guest of Honor at the World Fantasy Convention this year, and at GeyserCon in New Zealand 2019 and StokerCon 2019.

EJG: Thanks Kaaron! It was wonderful getting to know a bit more about you, and I'm sure many of us hope to see you at one of those upcoming conventions!

(February 3, 2018)

TIPS FOR FINALIZING YOUR SHORT STORY: AN ESSAY

BY KAARON WARREN

(*Author's note: I presented the following as part of a speech at Australia's University of Canberra in 2011. I've revised it slightly for this Primer).

I'VE BEEN WRITING SERIOUSLY SINCE ABOUT AGE fourteen. I sold my first story in 1993, after finding a flyer in the letterbox looking for feminist horror stories. I sold another early story after reading a small note looking for outré stories in a writer's magazine. I've been lucky, but I've also looked hard for my opportunities.

Since then, I've published over a hundred short stories, six short story collections, and four novels, with this Primer being my eleventh book.

I've always read voraciously. I imagine most of you are the same.

I've always loved reading and telling stories. I love solving mysteries and inventing characters, making them do interesting or depraved things.

I read *Grimm's Fairy Tales* from the age of five, a big huge book which surprised my grandmother. I loved the way those stories build the fright. You know something's coming and it does.

I have always read broadly. Fiction, non-fiction, magazines, newspapers. All of it can be of interest, and all of it has helped me get to a point where I have an 'instinct' for story.

You need this, to a certain extent, to finalize any piece of fiction you're working on. Novels, short stories, short shorts all require the same sort of finishing touches.

So how do you finish off a story?

Firstly, all those little 'notes to self' have to be incorporated or deleted. I usually end up with a page or two, headed *Are these points clear? Are they needed?* because I'm never sure until the end how much I can put into a story. You may have notes like "Finish this conversation" or "Mention the cat again" or "Don't forget she broke her arm". Make sure all of these are completed.

Secondly, go back to your original notes/thoughts when you started writing the piece. Have you expressed the original thought or have you travelled from it?

If it has travelled, does it matter? You know the old saying, "Kill your Darlings"? (Attributed to a number of people, including Faulkner and Quiller-Couch.)

What this saying means to me is not just about sentences you love that no longer fit the story, but that it means the way the story also develops. Sometimes it travels to unexpected places, which, to me, is a good thing. You want your story to move to a place your reader doesn't expect, as long as it makes a kind of sense. I really hate stories with surprise endings that come completely out of the blue at you, just for the sake of a surprise.

If you have travelled from your original idea, is it a better story this way? If it is, then move on! If not, you may have to reconsider the story. Try rewriting it from the point it veers away from your original idea and see where you end up. One writing technique is to write twenty different endings to a story, which really pushes creativity and definitely means you come up with unexpected ways to take the story.

Try to think logically. What should happen next? Is that how you want the story to end? Does it give you the result you were looking for? Then think *illogically* and ask the same questions.

One story of mine where this happened is "Coalescence", which is about a future where, at the moment of death, the frontal lobes of wealthy, highly intelligent and/or successful people are transplanted into the skulls of schizophrenic, destitute people. The idea being that the so-called successful people have more to give society than the so-called failures. It's a pretty cruel story.

It started off being an idea about religion and the transfer of belief, but shifted fairly quickly as I built the character, called Schizo Blogger. I was happy for this to happen, because I can always go back and tell that story about religion in a different way. So here, I let go of the original idea and went with the new one in the same setting.

The third thing to do when you've nearly finished your story is to read it aloud, even if it's a short piece. You mostly likely already do that. There still needs to be rhythm, even in a short story, and reading aloud will make sure you've got that rhythm. Also, it will help you find repetitive words. It'll also help ensure any dialogue you use sounds realistic and natural. Ellen Datlow, the American massively award-winning editor, says this is really important. Unnatural sounding dialogue can destroy a story. Ray Bradbury's dialogue is odd and stilted, to my ear, but it works for him. I don't think it works many other places.

Get someone else to read it to you. This can help you hear the flaws as well. This will also help make sure your first and last lines and paragraphs are absolute rippers. I think the last line is as important as the first: It must resonate. You want your reader to repeat that last line over and over. To be left hearing it.

It should make them want to read the story again.

For first lines, one of my favorites is from *The Go-Between* by L.P. Hartley: "The past is a foreign country: they do things differently there."

The first line from my story "Bone-Dog" doesn't match that, but the editor I submitted it to, Cat Sparks, still talks about the fact she bought the story based on this opening alone!

As for last lines, I love Harlan Ellison's "A Boy and his Dog". It ends simply, "A boy needs his dog", but it's the kind of ending line which makes you go right back to the beginning and read the story again.

My story "A Positive" ends this way: "I felt unwonted tenderness when they let Dad wander the grounds in his nightshirt, a small figure with a painted face, laughter drawn in red around his mouth. He stroked and patted every part of his body. I imagined he was memorizing it for the day it would be taken away from him completely."

Again, I hope it makes the reader want to go back to the start and read the story again straight away.

I like to listen to *The New Yorker* podcasts. I download them for free from iTunes. These are short stories that have appeared in the magazine, read by other writers who were inspired by them.

There are a lot of good ones, but also some bad. The thing that strikes me is that most of them could end anywhere; they have no clear finish. I don't mind that; I like the idea that stories are merely episodes in people's lives.

The best one I've heard there is called "Last Night", by James Salter. Speaking of ripper last paragraphs, this one is brilliant. Absolutely brilliant. Salter is a bit like Raymond Carver in the rest of his work. This story, to me, is far and away his best. Track it down if you can.

Next, be sure your story starts in the right place. Is it as compelling as possible? Or are you spending too much time setting the scene?

In a short piece, I'd say to remove most transportation stuff: *waking up*, *walking*, *driving*, unless it's important.

So many movies start with a ten minute driving scene. I hate it. They fill in with empty dialogue or music or scenery. Wasteful.

The read-aloud stage can also help you to remove dull words and replace them with active ones.

This, to me, is where the real difference of writing a novel versus writing a short story comes in. Not that in a novel you should use boring, inactive words, but you have a lot more room for word play. In a mini saga, or a short short, every single word has to count.

So consider, can you remove words such as:

- and
- then
- seems to
- about to
- kind of
- a little (*that's one of my big ones*)
- almost
- like

Additionally in a short, there is less room for "double words" that you might use for emphasis.

For example: *was strong, was hard and strong*. This sounds poetical, but it's perhaps too wordy when you only have a thousand or so words to play with.

Every word has to have one or more uses in a short short while moving forward many things: Imagery. Meaning. Plot. Character.

Next: The title is so important! Especially in a short short. You can tell part of your story in the title.

I already mentioned Harlan Ellison's "A Boy and His Dog". I think part of the story is told this way. Then there's Shirley

Jackson's "The Lottery", which is a wonderful story. The title sets you up for what might happen.

I don't think I'm very good at titles. I tend to use them as a description, whereas they can be used to far greater effect.

Some titles I've liked recently include "each thing I show you is a piece of my death" (sic) by Gemma Files, who also wrote the wonderful "The Emperor's Old Bones". Another title is by one of my favorite authors, Michael Marshall Smith: "What You See When You Wake Up in the Night".

Before you hand anything in, be brutally honest with yourself. Don't pretend it's good when it isn't. Make it better. It can be hard when you're sick to death of the thing, but if you know for a fact it isn't good enough, make it better. Your work is your record; make sure everything on your record is good.

To demonstrate some of the ways people are playing with short short fiction, I thought I'd talk about a short story competition I entered.

Christopher Fowler (another of my favorite authors) and Irish writer, Maureen Mchugh, were stirred to action by their irritation about the latest wave of so-called horror fiction, the mash-ups of classic fiction from Jane Austen and others with zombies, vampires, and werewolves. They think this form of fiction is de-horrifying horror, and I tend to agree.

They also decided they were tired of the torture porn movies. The horror of pure violence, they thought, was far from where they'd like horror to be.

So they launched a competition: five hundred words of horror. Complete short stories. They called it the *Campaign for Real Fear* and wanted to discover new monsters.

They had over five hundred entries. All were anonymous, which made it interesting as far as how many 'known' authors made it through, and also regarding the female/male ratio.

In the end, they chose twenty stories, which were published in the always brilliant *Black Static* magazine. There were more women than men selected, and there were only a couple of reasonably established authors. Gemma Files, the author of "The Emperor's New Bones", was one. I was another.

I was thrilled to win, because, being anonymous, I knew it had nothing to do with my 'name', whatever that means. It had only to do with the short story itself.

This is the story.

The Rude Little Girl

The rude little girl is back.

I was five when I last saw her forty years ago.

She was rude, and brave, too. I would never have dared to do what she did, climb up onto the lip of the underpass and let her feet dangle down.

"How did you get up there?" I shouted at her. She stared at me. Didn't answer. I stepped closer to shout again but she lifted herself and dropped down onto Greg's shoulders.

She clung there.

He didn't even flinch.

"Get off him!" I shouted. She stuck her tongue out at me and dug her fingers into his hair.

"Get off!" I shouted, pulling hard at her leg.

"Stop pinching!" Greg said. He shoved me, I shoved back and we had an all-out fight.

The girl clung around his neck, rolled with us. She was skinny as a stick. She winked at me.

"Get that girl off," I said.

"What girl? You're an idiot," Greg said.

I won the fight. He ran away, the girl's pigtails flapping. I never usually won.

He had already weakened.

The girl stuck with Greg for weeks, staring, smiling, and winking at me. No one else could see her. I told people there was a girl on Greg's back until they looked at me funny. That girl got fatter and fatter. When she was full she dropped off.

The next time I saw her she was skinny again. She sat on the lip of the underpass, staring, as the kids walked under. She smiled when she saw me.

I turned and ran, hid behind a tree, and she dropped onto Lisa, who was school captain and played every sport girls could play.

The rude girl got fatter. She was still on Lisa's shoulders when we moved, soon afterward.

Those children, those friends of mine, are still in the town, in the care of their parents. They never got old in the brain. Their bodies aged like mine did, but they have the minds of children. Keeping the rude girl company. There are others, too; research has been done, the syndrome named, to no avail.

This late child of ours, this glorious son, was an accident we both thank God for daily.

I thought the rude girl would leave me alone if I said nothing, did nothing. But she is back. She crouches at his cot like a gargoyle, waiting to pounce whenever he is laid down. So I carry him everywhere. My wife admonishes me, tells me to let him be. I can't leave him in her care. She doesn't see.

The rude little girl sits close by, blinking, and reaching out to pinch him now and again.

I can't get away from her. I tried running but she was waiting on lamp posts, a car roof.

Instead, we go to places children gather, tempt her with these others.

She will not have him as her companion.

I will not let him go.

Not even when he cries.

MEMENTO MORI

A BIBLIOGRAPHY OF

ENGLISH LANGUAGE FICTION

FOR KAARON WARREN

FOLLOWING IS A COMPLETE BIBLIOGRAPHY OF ENGLISH language fiction for Kaaron Warren through March, 2018. Not included are: foreign language translations, individual pieces of non-fiction, or individual pieces of poetry.

Abbreviations Used:

(1) = indicates story's first publication. Omitted if story first published in author collection.

(c) = indicates the collection containing this story. If the collection is listed first, the story's first appearance was in this collection.

(r) = indicates this is a reprint appearance.

anth. = anthology

mag. = magazine

f.c. = fiction collection

ed. = edited

v. = magazine volume number

= magazine issue number

SHORT FICTION

"68 Days"
> (1) *Tomorrow's Cthulhu: Stories at the Dawn of Posthumanity* (anth., ed. C. Dombrowski and Scott Gable): Broken Eye Books, 2016.

"A Positive" (var: "A-Positive")
> (1) *Bloodsongs* (mag., #10): Implosion Publishing, Winter 1998.
> (r) *Macabre: A Journey Through Australia's Darkest Fears* (anth., ed. Angela Challis and Marty Young): Brimstone Press, 2010.
> (c) *The Grinding House* (f.c.): CSFG Publishing, 2005.
> (c) *Dead Sea Fruit* (f.c.): Ticonderoga Publications, 2010.
> (c) *Cemetery Dance Select: Kaaron Warren* (f.c.): Cemetery Dance Publications, 2015.

"Air, Water and the Grove"
> (1) *The Lowest Heaven* (anth., ed. Anne C. Perry and Jared Shurin): Jurassic London, 2013.
> (r) *The Year's Best Dark Fantasy & Horror 2014 Edition* (anth., ed. Paula Guran): Prime Books, 2014.
> (r) *Focus 2013: Highlights of Australian Short Fiction* (anth., ed. Tehani Wessely): FableCroft Publishing, 2014.
> (c) *Cemetery Dance Select: Kaaron Warren* (f.c.): Cemetery Dance Publications, 2015.

"All Roll Over"
> (1) *In Your Face* (anth., ed. Tehani Wessely): FableCroft Publishing, 2016.

"All You Can Do Is Breathe"
> (1) *Blood and Other Cravings* (anth., ed. Ellen Datlow): Tor, 2011.
> (r) *The Year's Best Dark Fantasy & Horror 2012 Edition* (anth., ed. Paula Guran): Prime Books, 2012.
> (r) *The Year's Best Australian Fantasy & Horror 2011* (anth., ed. Liz Grzyb and Talie Helene): Ticonderoga Publications, 2012.

(r) *Nightmare Magazine* (online media): nightmare-mag.com, Oct. 2013.

(c) *Cemetery Dance Select: Kaaron Warren* (f.c.): Cemetery Dance Publications, 2015.

"**Al**'s Iso Bar"

(1) *The Alsiso Project* (anth., ed. Andrew Hook): Elastic Press, 2004.

(c) *The Grinding House* (f.c.): CSFG Publishing, 2005.

"**A**nother Week in the Future, An Excerpt"

(1) *Cranky Ladies of History* (anth., ed. Tansy Rayner Roberts and Tehani Wessely): FableCroft Publishing, 2015.

"**B**irthday"

(1) *AurealisXpress* (online media): aurealisblog.wordpress.com, Apr. 2002.

"**B**lame the Neighbours"

(1) *Slices of Flesh* (anth., ed. Stan Swanson): Dark Moon Books, 2012.

"**B**lood is Blood"

(1) *Twisted Histories* (anth., ed. Scott Harrison): Snowbooks, 2013.

"The **B**lue Stream"

(1) *Aurealis* (mag., #14): Chimaera Publications, Oct. 1994.

(r) *Dead Souls* (anth., ed. Mark S. Deniz): Morrigan Books, 2009.

(c) *The Grinding House* (f.c.): CSFG Publishing, 2005.

(c) *Cemetery Dance Select: Kaaron Warren* (f.c.): Cemetery Dance Publications, 2015.

"The **B**ody Finder"

(1) *Blurring the Line* (anth., ed. Marty Young): Cohesion Press, 2015.

(r) *The Dark* (e-mag., #12): TDM Press, May 2016.

(r) *The Year's Best Dark Fantasy & Horror 2016 Edition* (anth., ed. Paula Guran): Prime Books, 2016.

"**B**one-Dog"

(1) *Agog! Terrific Tales* (anth., ed. Cat Sparks): Agog! Press, 2003.

(c) *Dead Sea Fruit* (f.c.): Ticonderoga Publications, 2010.

(c) *The Glass Woman* (f.c.): Prime Books, 2007.

"The **B**one Mason"

(1) *Yog-Blogsoth* (online media): yog-blogsoth.blogspot.com, Aug. 2015.

"The **B**ook of the Climbing Lights"

(1) *The Starry Wisdom Library: The Catalogue of the Greatest Occult Book Auction of All Time* (anth., ed. Nate Pedersen): PS Publishing, 2014.

"**B**orn and Bread"

(1) *Once Upon a Time: New Fairy Tales* (anth., ed. Paula Guran): Prime Books, 2013.

(r) *The Year's Best Australian Fantasy & Horror 2013* (anth., ed. Liz Grzyb and Talie Helene): Ticonderoga Publications, 2014.

(c) *Exploring Dark Short Fiction #2: A Primer to Kaaron Warren* (f.c., ed. Eric J. Guignard): Dark Moon Books, 2018.

"**B**ridge of Sighs"

(1) *Fearful Symmetries* (anth., ed. Ellen Datlow): ChiZine Publications, 2014.

(r) *The Year's Best Australian Fantasy & Horror 2014* (anth., ed. Liz Grzyb and Talie Helene): Ticonderoga Publications, 2015.

"**B**uster and Corky"

(1) *Scary Food: A Compendium of Gastronomic Atrocity* (anth., ed. Cat Sparks): Agog! Press, 2008.

(c) *Dead Sea Fruit* (f.c.): Ticonderoga Publications, 2010.

"The **C**apture Diamonds"

(1) *Shadow Box* (anth., ed. Shane Jiraiya Cummings and Angela Challis): Brimstone Press, 2005.

(c) *Dead Sea Fruit* (f.c.): Ticonderoga Publications, 2010.

"The **C**ensus-Taker's Tale"

(1) *Canterbury 2100: Pilgrimages in a New World* (anth., ed. Dirk
   Flinthart): Agog! Press, 2008.
(r) *The Year's Best Australian Science Fiction and Fantasy (Fifth
   Annual Volume)* (anth., ed. Bill Congreve): MirrorDanse
   Books, 2010.
(c) *Dead Sea Fruit* (f.c.): Ticonderoga Publications, 2010.

"Coalescence"
   (1) *Aurealis* (mag., #37): Chimaera Publications, Mar. 2007.
   (c) *Dead Sea Fruit* (f.c.): Ticonderoga Publications, 2010.

"Cooling the Crows"
   (1) *In Bad Dreams, Volume One: Where Real Life Awaits* (anth., ed.
      Mark S. Deniz and Sharyn Lilley): Eneit Press, 2007.
   (c) *Dead Sea Fruit* (f.c.): Ticonderoga Publications, 2010.

"The Coral Gatherer"
   (c) *Dead Sea Fruit* (f.c.): Ticonderoga Publications, 2010.

"Creek"
   (c) *Through Splintered Walls* (f.c.): Twelfth Planet Press, 2012.

"Crisis Apparition"
   (c) *Exploring Dark Short Fiction #2: A Primer to Kaaron Warren*
      (f.c., ed. Eric J. Guignard): Dark Moon Books, 2018.

"Dead Sea Fruit"
   (1) *Fantasy Magazine* (mag., #4): Prime Books, Fall 2006.
   (r) *The Year's Best Fantasy and Horror: Twentieth Annual Collection*
      (anth., ed. Ellen Datlow, Kelly Link, and Gavin J. Grant): St.
      Martin's Griffin, 2007.
   (r) *The Year's Best Australian Science Fiction and Fantasy: (Third
      Annual Volume)* (anth., ed. Michelle Marquardt and Bill
      Congreve): MirrorDanse Books, 2007.
   (r) *Nightmares: A New Decade of Modern Horror* (anth., ed. Ellen
      Datlow): Tachyon Publications, 2016.
   (c) *Dead Sea Fruit* (f.c.): Ticonderoga Publications, 2010.
   (c) *The Gate Theory* (f.c.): Cohesion Press, 2013.

"**D**eath's Door Café"

(1) *Shadows & Tall Trees 5* (anth., ed. Michael Kelly): Undertow Publications, 2014.

(r) *Focus 2014: Highlights of Australian Short Fiction* (anth., ed. Tehani Wessely): FableCroft Publishing, 2015.

(r) *Nightmare Magazine* (online media): nightmare-mag.com, Apr. 2016.

(c) *Exploring Dark Short Fiction #2: A Primer to Kaaron Warren* (f.c., ed. Eric J. Guignard): Dark Moon Books, 2018.

"The **D**iesel Pool"

(1) *Cthulhu Deep Down Under: Volume 1* (anth., ed. Steve Proposch, Christopher Sequeira, and Bryce Stevens): IFWG Publishing Australia, 2017.

"**D**ig Dig Dig"

(1) *Noises in the Dark* (anth., ed. Paul Collins and Meredith Costain): Longman/ Pearson Education Australia, 2000.

"The **D**oll Beautician"

(1) *Review of Australian Fiction* (e-mag., v.17, #3): Review of Australian Fiction, Feb. 2016.

"**D**oll Money"

(1) *Fables and Reflections* (mag., #7): Fables and Reflections; Australia, Apr. 2005.

(r) *Devil Dolls and Duplicates In Australian Horror* (anth., ed. Anthony Ferguson): Equilibrium Books, 2011.

(c) *Dead Sea Fruit* (f.c.): Ticonderoga Publications, 2010.

"**D**own to the Silver Spirits"

(1) *Paper Cities: An Anthology of Urban Fantasy* (anth., ed. Ekaterina Sedia): Senses Five Press, 2008.

(r) *Unconventional Fantasy: A Celebration of Forty Years of the World Fantasy Convention* (anth., ed. Peggy Rae Sapienza, Jean Marie Ward, Bill Campbell, and Sam Lubell): Baltimore Washington Area Worldcon Association, Inc., 2014.

(c) *Dead Sea Fruit* (f.c.): Ticonderoga Publications, 2010.

"Eating the Alice Cake"
(1) *Mad Hatters and March Hares* (anth., ed. Ellen Datlow): Tor, 2017.

"The Edge of a Thing"
> (1) *The British Fantasy Society Yearbook 2009* (anth., ed. Guy Adams): The British Fantasy Society, 2009.
> (c) *Dead Sea Fruit* (f.c.): Ticonderoga Publications, 2010.

"Eleanor Atkins is Dead and Her House is Boarded Up"
> (1) *SQ Mag* (e-mag., #14): IFWG Publishing Australia, May 2014.
> (r) *Star Quake 3: SQ Mag's Best of 2014* (anth., ed. Sophie Yorkston): IFWG Publishing Australia, 2014.

"Ernestine's Senses"
> (1) *Whodunit? (Thrillogy series)* (anth., ed. Paul Collins and Meredith Costain): Longman/ Pearson Education Australia, 2001.

"Exceeding Bitter"
> (1) *Evil is a Matter of Perspective: An Anthology of Antagonists* (anth., ed. Adrian Collins and Mike Myers): Grimdark Magazine, 2017.

"Finding the Path"
> (1) *Thirteen* (Audio anth., ed. Scott Harrison): Spokenworld Audio/ Ladbroke Audio Ltd, 2013.

"The First Interview"
> (1) *Social Alternatives Magazine* (mag., v.14, #3): UQ, Apr. 1995.

"The Five Loves of Ishtar" (novella)
> (1) *Ishtar* (anth., ed. K. V. Taylor and Amanda Pillar): Gilgamesh Press, 2011.

"Fresh Young Widow"
> (c) *The Grinding House* (f.c.): CSFG Publishing, 2005.
> (r) *The Year's Best Australian Science Fiction and Fantasy (Second Annual Volume)* (anth., ed. Bill Congreve and Michelle Marquardt): MirrorDanse Books, 2006.

(r) *Australian Dark Fantasy and Horror: 2006 Edition* (anth., ed. Shane Jiraiya Cummings and Angela Challis): Brimstone Press, 2006.

(c) *Dead Sea Fruit* (f.c.): Ticonderoga Publications, 2010.

"**F**urtherest"

(1) *Dark Screams: Volume Seven* (anth., ed. Brian James Freeman and Richard Chizmar): Hydra/ Random House, 2017.

(r) *The Best Horror of the Year Volume 10* (anth., ed. Ellen Datlow): Night Shade Books, 2018.

"The **G**ate Theory"

(c) *The Gate Theory* (f.c.): Cohesion Press, 2013.

"The **G**aze Dogs of Nine Waterfall"

(1) *Exotic Gothic 3: Strange Visitations* (anth., ed. Danel Olson): Ash-Tree Press, 2009.

(r) *The Best Horror of the Year Volume 2* (anth., ed. Ellen Datlow): Night Shade Books, 2010.

(r) *Bewere the Night* (anth., ed. Ekaterina Sedia): Prime Books, 2011.

(c) *Dead Sea Fruit* (f.c.): Ticonderoga Publications, 2010.

(c) The Gate Theory (f.c.): Cohesion Press, 2013.

"**G**host Jail"

(1) *2012* (anth., ed. Ben Payne and Alisa Krasnostein): Twelfth Planet Press, 2008.

(r) *The Apex Book of World SF* (anth., ed. Lavie Tidhar): Apex Publications, 2009.

(r) *Never Again* (anth., ed. Allyson Bird and Joel Lane): Gray Friar Press, 2010.

(c) *Dead Sea Fruit* (f.c.): Ticonderoga Publications, 2010.

"The **G**ibbet Bell"

(1) *Borderlands* (mag., #8): Borderlands Publications, Oct. 2006.

(c) *Dead Sea Fruit* (f.c.): Ticonderoga Publications, 2010.

"That **G**irl"
(1) *Haunted Legends* (anth., ed. Ellen Datlow and Nick Mamatas): Tor, 2010.
(r) *The Year's Best Australian Fantasy & Horror 2010* (anth., ed. Liz Grzyb and Talie Helene): Ticonderoga Publications, 2011.
(c) *The Gate Theory* (f.c.): Cohesion Press, 2013.

"The **G**lass Woman"
(1) *Aurealis* (mag., #22): Chimaera Publications, Dec. 1998.
(c) *The Grinding House* (f.c.): CSFG Publishing, 2005.

"The **G**ossip Writer's Notebook"
(1) *CEA Greatest Anthology Written* (anth., ed. Shaun M. Jooste): Celenic Earth Publications, 2017.

"**G**reen"
(1) *Shadow Box* (anth., ed. Shane Jiraiya Cummings and Angela Challis): Brimstone Press, 2008.
(c) *Dead Sea Fruit* (f.c.): Ticonderoga Publications, 2010.

"The **G**rinding House" (novella)
(c) *The Grinding House* (f.c.): CSFG Publishing, 2005.
(c) *Dead Sea Fruit* (f.c.): Ticonderoga Publications, 2010.

"**G**uarding the Mound"
(1) *Encounters: An Anthology of Australian Speculative Fiction* (anth., ed. Maxine McArthur and Donna Maree Hanson): CSFG Publishing, 2004.
(c) *Dead Sea Fruit* (f.c.): Ticonderoga Publications, 2010.
(c) *Exploring Dark Short Fiction #2: A Primer to Kaaron Warren* (f.c., ed. Eric J. Guignard): Dark Moon Books, 2018.

"The **H**anging People"
(1) *Bloodsongs* (mag., #7): Bambada Press, 1996.
(c) *The Grinding House* (f.c.): CSFG Publishing, 2005.

"His Lipstick Minx"
>   (1) *The Workers' Paradise* (anth., ed. Russell B. Farr and Nick Evans): Ticonderoga Publications, 2007.
>
>   (c) *Dead Sea Fruit* (f.c.): Ticonderoga Publications, 2010.

"The History Thief" (novella)
>   (1) *Visions Fading Fast* (anth., ed. Gary McMahon): Pendragon Press, 2012.
>
>   (c) The Gate Theory (f.c.): Cohesion Press, 2013.

"Hive of Glass"
>   (1) *Baggage* (anth., ed. Gillian Polack): Eneit Press, 2010; (ebook): Wildside Press, 2015.

"Horrifea Nervosa"
>   (1) *100 Lightnings* (anth., ed. Stephen Studach): Paroxysm Press, 2015.

"The Human Moth"
>   (1) *The Grimscribe's Puppets* (anth., ed. Joseph S. Pulver, Sr.): Miskatonic River Press, 2013.

"In the Drawback"
>   (c) *The Grinding House* (f.c.): CSFG Publishing, 2005.
>
>   (c) Dead Sea Fruit (f.c.): Ticonderoga Publications, 2010.
>
>   (r) *Cthulhu: Deep Down Under* (anth., ed. Steve Proposch, Christopher Sequeira, and Bryce Stevens): Horror Australis, 2015.

"Investigation into an Accidental Death"
>   (1) *Tamba Magazine* (mag., #12): Goulburn Valley Writers' Group Inc., Autumn 1996.

"The Lantern Men"
>   (1) *Two Hundred and Twenty-One Baker Streets: An Anthology of Holmesian Tales Across Time and Space* (anth., ed. David Thomas Moore): Abaddon Books, 2014.

"The Left Behind"
>   (1) *Orb Speculative Fiction* (mag., #1): Orb Publications, Autumn-Winter 2000.
>   (c) *The Grinding House* (f.c.): CSFG Publishing, 2005.
>   (r) *Cemetery Dance* (mag., #69): Cemetery Dance Publications, Apr. 2013.

"The Lighthouse Keepers' Club"
>   (1) *Exotic Gothic 4 (Postscripts 28/29)* (anth., ed. Danel Olson): PS Publishing, 2012.

"The List of Definite Endings"
>   (1) *Teeth: Vampire Tales* (anth., ed. Ellen Datlow and Terri Windling): Harper (HarperCollins Publishers), 2011.

"Loss"
>   (1) *Sprawl* (anth., ed. Alisa Krasnostein): Twelfth Planet Press, 2010.

"Loud Music"
>   (1) *Spies, Lies and Watching Eyes* (anth., ed. Melissa Chan and J Terry): Artemis Press, 1995.

"Lucky Fingers"
>   (1) *Steampunk Cookbook* (anth., ed. Sharyn Lilley): Eneit Press, 2011.

"Mine Intercom"
>   (1) *Review of Australian Fiction* (e-mag., v.13, #6): Review of Australian Fiction, Mar. 2015.
>   (r) *The Year's Best Australian Fantasy & Horror 2015* (anth., ed. Liz Grzyb and Talie Helene): Ticonderoga Publications, 2017.

"The Missing Children"
>   (1) *There is No Mystery* (anth., ed. Kathy Kituai): Ginninderra Press, 1999.
>   (c) *The Grinding House* (f.c.): CSFG Publishing, 2005.

"Morace's Story" (novella)

> (1) (novella): Angry Robot, 2011 (NOTE: A children's version, tie-in to the novel, *Walking the Tree).*

"Mountain"

> (c) *Through Splintered Walls* (f.c.): Twelfth Planet Press, 2012.
>
> (r) *Nightmare Magazine* (online media): nightmare-mag.com, May 2015.

"My Smile"

> (1) *Nasty Snips* (anth., ed. Christopher C. Teague): MT Publishing, 1999.

"The Naked Man"

> (1) *Teratoid* (mag., #15): Teratoid, Autumn 1996.

"The New Rat in Town"

> (1) *Worlds Next Door* (anth., ed. Tehani Wessely): FableCroft Publishing, 2010.

"The Nursery Corner"

> (1) *Fearsome Magics* (anth., ed. Jonathan Strahan): Solaris, 2014.
>
> (r) *The Year's Best Dark Fantasy & Horror 2015 Edition* (anth., ed. Paula Guran): Prime Books, 2015.

"The Optimist"

> (1) *The Many Tortures of Anthony Cardno* (anth., ed. Anthony R. Cardno): Talekyn Press, 2014.

"The Paper Room"

> (1) *Going Down Swinging* (mag., #15): Going Down Swinging, 1995.

"Phylira Stands"

> (1) *Bestiary: Bizarre Myths and Chimerical Fancies* (anth., ed. Ellen Datlow): Viktor Koen Catalogue, 2015.

"The Pickwick Syndrome"

> (1) *Pandemonium: Stories of the Smoke* (anth., ed. Jared Shurin and Anne C. Perry): Jurassic London, 2012.

"Polish"
- (1) *Andromeda Spaceways Inflight Magazine* (mag., #28): Andromeda Spaceways Publishing Co-op, Apr. 2007.
- (r) *Best of ASIM vol. 2: Horror* (anth., ed. Juliet Bathory and Mark Farrugia): Andromeda Spaceways Publishing Co-op, 2010.
- (c) *Dead Sea Fruit* (f.c.): Ticonderoga Publications, 2010.

"A Pot to Piss In"
- (1) *Voices from the Past* (anth., ed. Scott Harrison and Lee Harris): H & H Books, 2011.

"The Public Menace of Blight"
- (1) *RiotACT* (online media: serial): the-riotact.com, Jan. 2016.
- (r) *The Refuge Collection Volume 3: More Tales from Refuge* (anth., ed. Steve Dillon): Oz Horror Con, 2016.
- (r) (chapbook): Steve Dillon, 2016.

"Purity"
- (1) *Scenes from the Second Storey* (anth., ed. Amanda Pillar and Pete Kempshall): Morrigan Books, 2010.
- (c) *The Gate Theory* (f.c.): Cohesion Press, 2013.

"The River of Memory" (var: River of Memory)
- (1) *Women on War: A Zombies vs Robots Anthology* (anth., ed. Jeff Conner): IDW Publishing, 2012.
- (r) *The Year's Best Australian Fantasy & Horror 2012* (anth., ed. Liz Grzyb and Talie Helene): Ticonderoga Publications, 2013.

"Road"
- (c) *Through Splintered Walls* (f.c.): Twelfth Planet Press, 2012.

"The Rude Little Girl"
- (1) *Black Static* (mag., #17): TTA Press, Jun./Jul. 2010.

"Salamander" (var: The Salamander)
- (1) *Don't Cross the Water and Other Warnings* (anth., ed. Melissa Chan and J Terry): Artemis Press, 1994.
- (c) *The Grinding House* (f.c.): CSFG Publishing, 2005.

"The **S**ameness of Birthdays"
>   (1) *Betrayals* (anth., ed. Heide Seaman): Ginninderra Press, 2002.
>   (c) *The Grinding House* (f.c.): CSFG Publishing, 2005.

"The **S**chool Fair"
>   (1) *Ghosts and Ghoulies* (anth., ed. Paul Collins and Meredith Costain): Longman/ Addison Wesley Longman Australia, 1999.

"**S**eeing Eye Dog"
>   (1) *Amazon Shorts* (online media): amazon.com/amazon-shorts-digital-shorts, 2008.

"**S**exual Trivia in Manhattan"
>   (1) *Razor* (mag., #1): Razor, 1997.

"**S**hadows of the Dead"
>   (1) *Sherlock Holmes The Australian Casebook: All new Holmes stories* (anth., ed. Christopher Sequeira): Echo, Bonnier Publishing Australia, 2017.

"**S**ick Cats in Small Spaces"
>   (1) *A World of Horror* (anth., ed. Eric J. Guignard): Dark Moon Books, 2018.

"**S**ins of the Ancestors"
>   (c) *Dead Sea Fruit* (f.c.): Ticonderoga Publications, 2010.
>   (c) *Exploring Dark Short Fiction #2: A Primer to Kaaron Warren* (f.c., ed. Eric J. Guignard): Dark Moon Books, 2018.

"**S**kin Holes"
>   (1) *Strange Fruit: Tales of the Unexpected* (anth., ed. Paul Collins): Penguin Books Australia, 1995.
>   (c) *The Grinding House* (f.c.): CSFG Publishing, 2005.

"**S**ky" (novella)
>   (c) *Through Splintered Walls* (f.c.): Twelfth Planet Press, 2012.
>   (r) *Focus 2012: Highlights of Australian Short Fiction* (anth., ed. Tehani Wessely): FableCroft Publishing, 2013.

"Sleeping with the Bower Birds"
    (1) *Shivers VII* (anth., ed. Richard Chizmar): Cemetery Dance Publications, 2013.
    (r) *The Best of Shivers* (anth., ed. Richard Chizmar): Cemetery Dance Publications, 2017.

"The Smell of Mice"
    (c) *The Grinding House* (f.c.): CSFG Publishing, 2005.

"Smoko"
    (c) *The Grinding House* (f.c.): CSFG Publishing, 2005.

"The Softening"
    (1) *Shadowed Realms* (e-mag., #9): Brimstone Press, Jan./Feb. 2006.
    (c) *Dead Sea Fruit* (f.c.): Ticonderoga Publications, 2010.

"The Speaker of Heaven"
    (1) *Orb Speculative Fiction* (mag., #2): Orb Publications, 2001.
    (r) *Orb Speculative Fiction (Best Of)* (mag., #8): Orb Publications, 2010.
    (c) *The Grinding House* (f.c.): CSFG Publishing, 2005.

"State of Oblivion"
    (1) *Elsewhere: An Anthology of Incredible Places* (anth., ed. Michael Barry): CSFG Publishing, 2003.
    (c) *Dead Sea Fruit* (f.c.): Ticonderoga Publications, 2010.
    (c) *Cemetery Dance Select: Kaaron Warren* (f.c.): Cemetery Dance Publications, 2015.

"Summer Coming"
    (1) *Narcissus Magazine* (mag., #10): ANU, 1994.

"Survival of the Last"
    (1) *Aurealis* (mag., #27/28): Chimaera Publications, Oct. 2001.
    (c) *The Grinding House* (f.c.): CSFG Publishing, 2005.

"Talent Napped"
    (1) *Forensics: Double Helix Science Kit* (Educational Interactive Science Kit, Manufactured under CSIRO): CSIRO Publishing, 2006.

"The Tell"
> (1) *Poe: 19 New Tales of Suspense, Dark Fantasy and Horror* (anth., ed. Ellen Datlow): Solaris, 2009.
>
> (r) *Australian Reader (Online Poe Celebration Issue)* (e-mag.): Australian Reader, 2009.

"The Tide" with Carol Ryles, Lezli Robyn, Daniel I. Russell, Felicity Dowker, Patty Jansen, Andrew J. McKiernan, Devin Jeyathurai, Alan Baxter, Martin Livings, and Chuck McKenzie
> (1) *Dead Red Heart: Australian Vampire Tales* (anth., ed. Russell B. Farr): Ticonderoga Publications, 2011.

"Tiger Kill"
> (1) *Earwig Flesh Factory* (mag., #3/4): Eraserhead Press, Fall/Winter 2000.
>
> (r) *Tails of Wonder and Imagination* (anth., ed. Ellen Datlow): Night Shade Books, 2010.
>
> (c) *The Grinding House* (f.c.): CSFG Publishing, 2005.

"Tontine Mary"
> (1) *New Ceres Nights* (anth., ed. Alisa Krasnostein and Tehani Wessely): Twelfth Planet Press, 2009.
>
> (c) Dead Sea Fruit (f.c.): Ticonderoga Publications, 2010.

"The Unwanted Women of Surrey"
> (1) *Queen Victoria's Book of Spells* (anth., ed. Ellen Datlow and Terri Windling): Tor, 2013.

"The Wandering Widget"
> (1) *Forensics Kit Education Pack* (Educational Interactive Science Kit, Manufactured under CSIRO): CSIRO Publishing, 1996.

"We Are All Bone Inside"
> (1) *Looming Low: Volume I* (anth., ed. Justin Steele and Sam Cowan): Dim Shores, 2017.

"White Bed"
> (1) *Shrieks: A Horror Anthology* (anth., ed. Jillian Bartlett, Cathi Joseph, and Anne Lawson): Women's Redress Press, 1993.

(r) *In Fabula-Divino* (anth., ed. Nicole Murphy): eMergent Publishing, 2013.

"The **W**hite Car"
>(1) *100 Lightnings* (anth., ed. Stephen Studach): Paroxysm Press, 2015.

"The **W**hither"
>(1) *Darker Companions* (anth., ed. Scott David Aniolowski and Joseph S. Pulver, Sr.): PS Publishing, 2017.

"**W**itnessing"
>(1) *The Canary Press Story Magazine* (mag., #6): The Canary Press, Dec. 2014.

"**W**oman Train"
>(1) *The Outcast: An Anthology of Exiles and Strangers* (anth., ed. Nicole R. Murphy): CSFG Publishing, 2006.
>(c) *Dead Sea Fruit* (f.c.): Ticonderoga Publications, 2010.

"**W**orking for the God of the Love of Money"
>(1) *Dark Regions* (mag., #16): Dark Regions Press, Fall 2001.
>(c) *The Grinding House* (f.c.): CSFG Publishing, 2005.

"The **W**rong Seat"
>(1) *Calling Up the Devil and Associated Misdemeanours* (anth., ed. Melissa Chan and J Terry): Artemis Press, 1994.
>(c) *The Grinding House* (f.c.): CSFG Publishing, 2005.
>(c) *Exploring Dark Short Fiction #2: A Primer to Kaaron Warren* (f.c., ed. Eric J. Guignard): Dark Moon Books, 2018.

"A **Y**ear in the Life"
>(1) *Refractory Girl Magazine* (mag., #15): Refractory Girl Collective, Spring 1996.

NOVELS, CHAPBOOKS, and OTHER SINGLE WORKS

The Grief Hole (novel): SQ Mag, 2016; (ebook): IFWG Publishing Incorporated, 2016.

Mistification (novel): Angry Robot, 2011.

The Public Menace of Blight (chapbook): Steve Dillon, 2016.

Slights (novel): Angry Robot, 2009.

Tide of Stone (novel): Omnium Gatherum, 2018.

Walking the Tree (novel): Angry Robot, 2010.

Morace's Story (novella, ebook): Angry Robot, 2011 (NOTE: A children's version, tie-in to the novel, *Walking the Tree)*.

COLLECTIONS

The Grinding House (fiction collection): CSFG Publishing, 2005.
    (r) (var: *The Glass Woman*) (fiction collection, including one additional story, "Bone-Dog"): Prime Books, 2007.

Cemetery Dance Select: Kaaron Warren (fiction collection): Cemetery Dance Publications, 2015.

Dead Sea Fruit (fiction collection): Ticonderoga Publications, 2010.

Exploring Dark Short Fiction #2: A Primer to Kaaron Warren (fiction collection, ed. Eric J. Guignard): Dark Moon Books, 2018.

Through Splintered Walls (Twelve Planets Book 6) (fiction collection): Twelfth Planet Press, 2012.

The Gate Theory (fiction collection): Cohesion Press, 2013.
    (r) IFWG Publishing Australia (SQ Mag), 2017.

MAGAZINES AS EDITOR

Midnight Echo (#11): Australian Horror Writers' Association, Apr. 2015.

ALSO FROM ERIC J. GUIGNARD AND DARK MOON BOOKS:

Every nation of the globe has unique tales to tell, whispers that settle in through the land, creatures or superstitions that enliven the night, but rarely do readers get to experience such a diversity of these voices in one place as in *A WORLD OF HORROR*, the latest anthology book created by award-winning editor Eric J. Guignard, and beautifully illustrated by artist Steve Lines.

Enclosed within its pages are twenty-two all-new dark and speculative fiction stories written by authors from around the world that explore the myths and monsters, fables and fears of their homelands.

Encounter the haunting things that stalk those radioactive forests outside Chernobyl in Ukraine; sample the curious dishes one may eat in Canada; beware the veldt monster that mirrors yourself in Uganda; or simply battle mountain trolls alongside Alfred Nobel in Sweden. These stories and more are found within *A World of Horror*: Enter and discover, truly, there's no place on the planet devoid of frights, thrills, and wondrous imagination.

> "This is the book we need right now! Fresh voices from all over the world, bringing American audiences new ways to feel the fear. Horror is a universal genre and for too long we have only experienced one western version of it. No more. Get ready to experience a whole new world of terror."
> —*Becky Spratford; librarian, reviewer,* RA for All: Horror

Order your copy at www.darkmoonbooks.com or www.amazon.com
ISBN-13: 978-0-9989383-1-8

ALSO FROM ERIC J. GUIGNARD AND DARK MOON BOOKS:

**Exploring Dark Short Fiction #1:
A Primer to Steve Rasnic Tem**

For over four decades, Steve Rasnic Tem has been an acclaimed author of horror, weird, and sentimental fiction. Hailed by *Publishers Weekly* as "A perfect balance between the bizarre and the straight-forward" and *Library Journal* as "One of the most distinctive voices in imaginative literature," Steve Rasnic Tem has been read and cherished the world over for his affecting, genre-crossing tales.

Dark Moon Books and editor Eric J. Guignard bring you this introduction to his work, the first in a series of primers exploring modern masters of literary dark short fiction. Herein is a chance to discover—or learn more of—the rich voice of Steve Rasnic Tem, as beautifully illustrated by artist Michelle Prebich.

Included within these pages are:

- Six short stories, one written exclusively for this book
- Author interview
- Complete bibliography
- Academic commentary by Michael Arnzen, PhD (former humanities chair and professor of the year, Seton Hill University)
- . . . and more!

Enter this doorway to the vast and fantastic: Get to know Steve Rasnic Tem.

ALSO FROM ERIC J. GUIGNARD AND DARK MOON BOOKS:

Exploring Dark Short Fiction #3: A Primer to Nisi Shawl

Praised by both literary journals and leading fiction magazines, Nisi Shawl is celebrated as an author whose works are lyrical and philosophical, speculative and far-ranging; "... broad in ambition and deep in accomplishment" (*The Seattle Times*). Besides nearly three decades of creating fantasy and science fiction, fairy tales, and indigenous stories, Nisi has also been lauded as editor, journalist, and proponent of feminism, African-American fiction, and other pedagogical issues of diversity.

Dark Moon Books and editor Eric J. Guignard bring you this introduction to her work, the third in a series of primers exploring modern masters of literary dark short fiction. Herein is a chance to discover—or learn more of—the vibrant voice of Nisi Shawl, as beautifully illustrated by artist Michelle Prebich.

Included within these pages are:

- Six short stories, one written exclusively for this book
- Author interview
- Complete bibliography
- Academic commentary by Michael Arnzen, PhD (former humanities chair and professor of the year, Seton Hill University)
- ... and more!

Enter this doorway to the vast and fantastic: Get to know Nisi Shawl.

ALSO FROM ERIC J. GUIGNARD AND DARK MOON BOOKS:

In this anthology, *DARK TALES OF LOST CIVILIZATIONS*, you will unearth twenty-five previously unpublished horror and speculative fiction stories relating to aspects of civilizations that are crumbling, forgotten, rediscovered, or perhaps merely spoken about in great and fearful whispers.

What is it that lures explorers to distant lands where none have returned? Where is Genghis Khan buried? What happened to Atlantis? Who will displace mankind on Earth? What laments have the Witches of Oz? Answers to these mysteries and other tales are presented within this critically acclaimed anthology.

"The stories range from mildly disturbing to downright terrifying… Most are written in a conservative, suggestive style, relying on the reader's own imagination to take the plunge from speculation to horror."

—*Monster Librarian Reviews*

"Several of these stories made it on to my best of the year shortlist, and the book itself is now on the best anthologies of the year shortlist."

—*British Fantasy Society*

"Almost any story in this anthology is worth the price of purchase. The entire collection is a delight."

—*Black Gate Magazine*

ALSO FROM ERIC J. GUIGNARD AND DARK MOON BOOKS:

Death. Who has not considered their own mortality and wondered at what awaits, once our frail human shell expires? What occurs after the heart stops beating, after the last breath is drawn, after life as we know it terminates?

Does our spirit remain on Earth while the body rots? Do the remnants of our soul transcend to a celestial Heaven or sink to Hell's torment? Can we choose our own afterlife? Can we die again in the hereafter? Are we given the opportunity to reincarnate and do it all over? Is life merely a cosmic joke or is it an experiment for something greater? Enclosed in this Bram Stoker-award winning anthology are thirty-four all-new dark and speculative fiction stories exploring the possibilities *AFTER DEATH . . .*

"Though the majority of the pieces come from the darker side of the genre, a solid minority are playful, clever, or full of wonder. This strong and well-themed anthology is sure to make readers contemplative even while it creates nightmares."

—*Publishers Weekly*

"In Eric J. Guignard's latest anthology he gathers some of the biggest and most talented authors on the planet to give us their take on this entertaining and perplexing subject matter . . . highly recommended."

—*Famous Monsters of Filmland*

"An excellent collection of imaginative tales of what waits beyond the veil."

—*Amazing Stories Magazine*

Order your copy at www.darkmoonbooks.com or www.amazon.com
ISBN-13: 978-0-9885569-2-8

ALSO FROM ERIC J. GUIGNARD AND DARK MOON BOOKS:

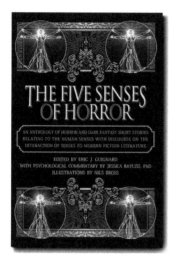

Hearing, sight, touch, smell, and taste: Our impressions of the world are formed by our five senses, and so too are our fears, our imaginations, and our captivation in reading fiction stories that embrace these senses.

Whether hearing the song of infernal caverns, tasting the erotic kiss of treachery, or smelling the lush fragrance of a fiend, enclosed within this anthology are fifteen horror and dark fantasy tales that will quicken the beat of fear, sweeten the flavor of wonder, sharpen the spike of thrills, and otherwise brighten the marvel of storytelling that is found resonant!

Editor Eric J. Guignard and psychologist Jessica Bayliss, PhD also include companion discourse throughout, offering academic and literary insight as well as psychological commentary examining the physiology of our senses, why each of our senses are engaged by dark fiction stories, and how it all inspires writers to continually churn out ideas in uncommon and invigorating ways.

Featuring stunning interior illustrations by Nils Bross, and including fiction short stories by such world-renowned authors as John Farris, Ramsey Campbell, Poppy Z. Brite, Darrell Schweitzer, and Richard Christian Matheson, amongst others.

Intended for readers, writers, and students alike, explore *THE FIVE SENSES OF HORROR*!

Order your copy at www.darkmoonbooks.com or www.amazon.com
ISBN-13: 978-0-9988275-0-6

THE CRIME FILES OF KATY GREEN by GENE O'NEILL:

Discover why readers have been applauding this stark, fast-paced noir series by multiple-award-winning author, Gene O'Neill, and follow the dark murder mysteries of Sacramento homicide detectives Katy Green and Johnny Cato, dubbed by the press as Sacramento's "Green Hornet and Cato"!

Book #1: *DOUBLE JACK* (a novella)

400-pound serial killer Jack Malenko has discovered the perfect cover: He dresses as a CalTrans worker and preys on female motorists in distress in full sight of passing traffic. How fast can Katy Green and Johnny Cato track him down before he strikes again?

Book #2: *SHADOW OF THE DARK ANGEL*

Bullied misfit, Samuel Kubiak, is visited by a dark guardian angel who helps Samuel gain just vengeance. There hasn't been a case yet Katy and Johnny haven't solved, but now how can they track a psychopathic suspect that comes and goes in the shadows?

Book #3: *DEATHFLASH*

Billy Williams can see the soul as it departs the body, and is "commanded to do the Lord's work," which he does fanatically, slaying drug addicts in San Francisco... Katy and Johnny investigate the case as junkies die all around, for Billy has his own addiction: the rush of viewing the Deathflash.

Order your copy at www.darkmoonbooks.com or www.amazon.com

ABOUT EDITOR, ERIC J. GUIGNARD

ERIC J. GUIGNARD IS A writer, editor, and publisher of dark and speculative fiction, operating from the shadowy outskirts of Los Angeles. He's won the Bram Stoker Award, been a finalist for the International Thriller Writers Award, and a multi-nominee of the Pushcart Prize.

His stories and non-fiction have appeared in publications such as *Nightmare Magazine, Black Static, Shock Totem, Buzzy Magazine,* and *Dark Discoveries Magazine.* As editor, Eric's published the anthologies *Dark Tales of Lost Civilizations, After Death...,* +*Horror Library*+ *Volume 6,* and is scheduled to release three more this year, including *A World of Horror,* a showcase of international horror short fiction.

Read his novella *Baggage of Eternal Night* (JournalStone) and watch for forthcoming books, including the novel *Crossbuck 'Bo.*

Outside the glamorous and jet-setting world of indie fiction, Eric's a technical writer and college professor, and he stumbles home each day to a wife, children, cats, and a terrarium filled with mischievous beetles. Visit Eric at: www.ericjguignard.com, his blog: ericjguignard.blogspot.com, or Twitter: @ericjguignard.

ABOUT ACADEMIC, MICHAEL ARNZEN, PHD

MICHAEL A. ARNZEN (PhD, University of Oregon, 1999) teaches full-time at Seton Hill University, home of the country's only MFA degree in Writing Popular Fiction. To date he has won four Bram Stoker Awards and an International Horror Critics Guild Award for his often funny, always disturbing horror fiction and poetry,  which includes such book-length titles as *Grave Markings*, *Play Dead*, *Freakcidents*, and *Proverbs for Monsters*. Alongside Heidi Ruby Miller, Arnzen also co-edited *Many Genres, One Craft: Lessons in Writing Popular Fiction*—a large how-to guide for authors of speculative fiction and other genres. Arnzen continues to write horror and criticism while teaching the zombie populations near Pittsburgh, PA. Follow Mike at http://michaelarnzen.com.

On top of his genre writing, Arnzen sits on the editorial board for *Paradoxa: Studies in World Literary Genres*, and his academic criticism has appeared in such journals as *Narrative*, *The Journal of Popular Film and Television*, and the *Journal of the Fantastic in the Arts*. An updated version of his doctoral dissertation—a critical survey of Freud's "unheimlich" in pop culture, called *The Popular Uncanny*—is forthcoming from Guide Dog Books. He maintains an irregular blog on the subject at http://gorelets.com/uncanny.

Early in his career, Arnzen lived in Colorado, where he became acquainted with Steve Rasnic Tem and other Western writers circulating in the orbit of genre legend Ed Bryant. Tem eventually selected Arnzen's story about the Royal Gorge for the classic Colorado spec-fic anthology, *High Fantastic* (1995) and Mike recalls learning a life-long editorial lesson from the experience that he will never forget: Always consider cutting your last sentence after finishing up a piece.

ABOUT ILLUSTRATOR, MICHELLE PREBICH

MICHELLE PREBICH IS A freelance artist who studied Film Production, Theatre, and Fine Art at Cal-State Long Beach. A film and literature geek, she loves the dark/romantic era and existential themes.

She has worked as a production designer, artist, set dresser, property master, and special effects makeup artist on short films, television segments, and web series for the film industry. Her collaboration with the band *Mr. Moonshine* includes art for their album and direction/design on two stop motion animation music videos. Her art he has been featured in galleries including Melt Down Comics and The Mystic Museum.

She sells original macabre art, art pieces, and apparel she has created through her shop "Bat in Your Belfry," which can be found at batinyourbelfry.etsy.com and on Instagram @batinyourbelfry. She loves geeking out with fellow enthusiasts of the unusual and macabre and can be typically found at Halloween/horror conventions usually standing next to a man in a cowboy hat.

CPSIA information can be obtained
at www.ICGtesting.com
Printed in the USA
FSHW02n0557250818
51604FS